Marion Brunet, born in 1976 in the Vaucluse, is a well known Young Adult author in France. Her YA novels have received over 30 prizes, including the 2017 UNICEF Prize for Youth Literature. Marion has previously worked as a special needs educator and now writes her fiction in Marseille. *Summer of Reckoning* is her first novel written for adults and her first work to be translated into English. It was the winner of the 2018 Grand Prix de Littérature Policière, the prestigious French crime fiction prize.

SUMMER OF RECKONING

Marion Brunet

Translated by Katherine Gregor

BITTER LEMON PRESS
LONDON

BITTER LEMON PRESS

First published in the United Kingdom in 2020 by
Bitter Lemon Press, 47 Wilmington Square, London WC1X 0ET

www.bitterlemonpress.com

First published in French in 2018 as
L'ÉTÉ CIRCULAIRE by Editions Albin Michel, Paris

A CIP record for this book is available from the British Library

ISBN 978–1–912242–269
eBook ISBN 978–1–912242–276

Bitter Lemon Press gratefully acknowledges the financial assistance of
the Arts Council of England and the Centre National du Livre.

Typeset by Tetragon, London
Printed and bound in Great Britain by Clays Ltd, Elcograf S.p.A.

To my sister

Then, no doubt responding to her own thought, she added, "You see, life is never as good or as bad as we think."

Guy de Maupassant, A Life

Bitch

At home, Johanna remembers, a hand on the backside was friendly, like – a way of saying you had a nice one, meaning "You've got potential" – something between a caress and a slap on the rump of a mare. The girls held trump cards, like in a tarot game, and you could almost say that if they played them right, they'd win. Except that neither of them – not Jo and not her sister Céline – have ever won any game. But since they hadn't drawn up the rules of the game, they were shafted whatever they did. Trump cards or bait, it was dead in the water before it even started.

For Céline, it's not a hand on her backside tonight, but a slap across her face. Her father, furious, is almost choking on his anger. He doesn't exactly have a wide range of vocabulary as it is, but this is worse. He turns his daughter's face with his huge builder's hand; she crashes down onto the kitchen floor – a heap of wet cloth. She makes an odd kind of sound, as though some bits of her have broken.

"*Who* is it?"

Céline couldn't answer even if she wanted to. She tries to catch her breath. Her hair hangs straight over her face, so you can't see her eyes or her mouth. Jo would like to help her but it's as though her feet are screwed to the floor like a prison bed.

The kitchen smells of detergent and lavender, like an advert for the South of France, cicadas and all.

"Who's the piece of shit that did this to you? Who's the son of a bitch who dared?"

Their mother fills a glass with water. It slips out of her hand and rolls into the stainless-steel sink. She whispers *Stop it*, but without conviction. Actually, you don't really know who she's saying it to.

"Are you going to answer me or not?"

Then her father stops yelling. His chin starts to quiver and that's even more threatening, so Jo looks away. Their mother crouches down, holding the glass of water, and lifts Céline's face but with no tenderness. She's never been shown any herself, after all. Just for a second, you wonder if she's about to throw the water in her daughter's face or help her drink it. Céline props herself up on the floor with one hand and clings to her mother with the other. The water spills and runs down her mother's bare knee and she gets annoyed, pulls away, leaves the glass on the floor and stands back up with difficulty – a very old woman all of a sudden, though she always carries on as if she's thirty. Céline lets go of her wrist and remains lying on her elbow. Her lip has swollen up and her nose looks crooked. Her father has never hit her so hard before. She takes the glass to drink from it but the water runs down the side, over her chin and onto her T-shirt that has a pink pattern with sequins around it, and there's blood bubbling out of her right nostril. There's a stabbing pain in her stomach, like a thousand darts.

Her father stands with his arms crossed, having regained his strength even in his body language, and challenges

Céline with his glare. Her eyes are full of water, her cheeks hollow from gritting her teeth.

"She's not going to tell," her mother hisses. "The bitch isn't going to tell us anything."

Freed from Desire

They'd looked almost attractive when they left home earlier that evening. The mother, with her carrot-orange tan and her skin glowing with lotion, wore her gold chain with the dolphin charm. She looked so young nibbling at the animal with her front teeth, smiling absent-mindedly. The father smelled of soap and aftershave and was breathing heavily. He quickly put his soft packet of Marlboros in his shirt pocket – the collar was already drenched in sweat – and lit a cigarette in the early evening. He squinted in the still-bright, purplish light. He looked at the rows of vines as though he owned them.

Like at the start of every summer, Céline was revealing her indecent beauty with outfits that were too tight, her denim shorts cut so high the fold between her buttocks and thighs opened and closed with every step she took.

As for Jo, she couldn't care less about what she was wearing; like every year since forever, she was going to a funfair feeling vaguely disgusted that she still found it somewhat exciting despite herself. So her skinny jeans dirty at the knees and black, shapeless tank top were good enough. She hung on her sister's shoulder like dead algae. "Why can't we take the car?"

Nobody replied. You could hear the bass thumping in the distance; it was a ten-minute walk at most.

The four of them were walking along the edge of the road together, a rare event. The girls picked up the pace to put some distance between them and their parents, the way they used to when they were little kids. Blades of dry grass penetrated their sandals and prickled their toes. They hopped on one foot and held on to each other's shoulders to remove them. When they were in sight of the fair, walking past the stone cross, they slowed down a little so the others crowding around the rides wouldn't think they were too impatient.

The village had been transformed: the funfair, set up for three days, altered the streets and offered contagious ecstasy and the smell of hot oil as far as the small central square right next to the church. The mother and father went up to the bar; the father's mates and their wives were already there. There was loud, buoyant laughter. Patrick was trying to get his wife to dance but she was giggling and yelling that she didn't feel like it and that he was already too drunk. They looked all lovey-dovey; you almost couldn't tell any more that he'd smashed in her face the week before. She looked like a large moth, wriggling in her blue dress. The women ordered some rosé and the men pastis. They said hello to the girls, who didn't linger.

"Better start keeping an eye on your eldest," Patrick's wife said with a grimace suggesting envy.

The father smiled proudly, his eyes following Céline's small backside. Sixteen and promising. Patrick cleared his throat and ordered another drink.

The same people coming together again, like every year, gangs and families who ignore one another or blend in with the crackling and chaos of the entertainment. Once a year. Of course, there's always St John's Eve and the school fete. But the fair is a lot more fun. Céline, the belle of the ball, adulated by the boys – never mind from which gang – has always loved it. Even when she was younger, there were shady corners where she could rub up against a boyfriend's body, playing at not going any further but stopping at the very edge. As for the boys, they'd dream of her pink fingernails on their erect little dicks; she would lovingly clutch large cuddly toys won in the shooting gallery, hoping for words of love. And if she had to let her breasts be clumsily fondled so she could obtain a miserable, stuttering *I love you* and other unimaginative derivatives, then she was up for it. She did want it, a little. Jo would be on the lookout.

But this evening, only her sister could see that Céline was pretending, opening her throat to laugh at Lucas's nonsense, at Enzo's half-baked jokes. She sparkled for the gallery.

They went to the Tarantula with the others. This ride first came here ten years ago, with its aluminium cars flashing red and yellow, small lights flickering to "Freed from Desire". Vertigo, as always, and the screams when the metal structure starts and lifts the clusters of willing flyers. Even old folks find it entertaining to watch youngsters get up there to give themselves a fright. Nobody's ever seemed to find it odd that the same dance track is played year after year, as though time had stopped in 1996, twenty years earlier.

Céline and Jo know it by heart. They've lost count of the number of times they've screamed all the way up there when the seats start turning slowly on themselves before falling down at a crazy speed then going back up as fast. But they keep coming back, for the thrill of it.

Lucas was already trying to overtake Enzo so he could get in with Céline.

She slid her hand across the nape of her neck to flick her hair back and time stood still in the eyes of the boys, between the lift and the slap as her hair cascaded down again. After that they started to breathe once more, a little less cocky but much braver than earlier, and with a slightly idiotic smile. But despite the game, despite the others, despite the pleasure of the sound being turned up to maximum – so you had to shout or glue your lips to the edge of an ear – the euphoria was just pretence. There was already this thing inside her which she was still pretending not to know about: a logical consequence, a cold logic that says trouble breeds nothing but trouble. She was still lying a little to herself, long enough for a ride, long enough to see two guys fight for the privilege of holding her tight by the waist while dizzy, absorbing her terrified screams and tangled hair as the machine descended, and hoping for more. And yet even as she turned to look at the large iron spider, her feet on the steps streaked with flashing colours, she felt sick. It was absurd: she wasn't afraid of the void, or the speed, and she'd always loved the rides. A kind of clammy oppressiveness – perhaps primeval intuition?

Céline turned to Enzo and her eyes appointed him for the first ride. Lucas was disappointed, but there would be others; they usually took ten rides a night at the funfair, and the evening was only just starting. The man with the first move didn't necessarily win the chess game. He stepped away to roll a joint. The next ride would be his. Vanessa was clinging to Manon, unless it was the other way around. They were giggling, pushing away Antony, who was embracing them and whispering stuff in their ears they were pretending not to understand. They were shaking their heads and their hips. Their eyes were shining. The music saturated the air around them, made the ground vibrate and travelled up their legs – *Want more and more, people just want more and more* – even Jo's. Her knees were vibrating slightly and she couldn't tell exactly if she liked this kind of frenzy or hated it. Her eyes travelled from the cars, finally emptied, to her sister. "You sure you're all right?" she said, forced to shout. Céline didn't answer. She looked white as a sheet, eyes dilated by the hysterical lights. She nodded, kept her head down, hair over her face. "You don't have to if you don't feel well," Jo continued. "It's not like every time we have to make do with the same ride we've had for the past ten years."

This managed to make Céline laugh. She bent down to scratch a mosquito bite on her calf. When she straightened up again she felt everything spinning, white dots in front of her eyes. Sweat bathed the back of her neck, already clammy with that mane of hair – she should have put it in a ponytail – and the beginning of summer. And then the crowd, the noise, the engine heat rising from the machine…

"Come on," Jo insisted, "let's get out of here. You look like shit."

"OK, back off. Have you seen yourself?"

"Fuck you, Céline. Go ahead, take the ride, you'll just throw up all over Enzo, bet he'll love that."

"What did you say?" Enzo shouted.

"Nothing," they replied in unison, not looking at him.

The music started again, grafted to the spider like the call of an animal. In a loop, irreversibly stuck on repeat. It occurred to Jo that she was the only one to grasp the irony of the situation.

They stepped into the cars. Jo sat first and pulled down the safety barrier. She always preferred to take her adrenaline injections alone. The others got in two by two, in giggling pairs, fastened the straps over their bellies and handed their plastic tokens to Sauveur, the manager of the ride: it's always been him, only now he has a tooth missing and thinner hair. He winked at Jo; he's always been good at spotting the oddballs, and loves them like a brother.

The spider got going, lifting its legs to the sky. Jo looked down: the kids were pressing their noses to the glass tanks piled up with miniature soft toys, trying to catch a rabbit with pincers, losing it every time. Further away, the bar and its display of glasses looked like a toy tea set and her parents like little animals.

"Freed from Desire" reverberated even louder up there.

This lurch above the world was suddenly intoxicating. Jo had forgotten. She would have preferred a different soundtrack, something grandiose or coarse instead of this old-fashioned crap. Never mind; she enjoyed the spin and her legs feeling like cotton wool. It's so fucking boring here that any strong emotion will do. At least if they shudder it means they're not dead, stuck on repeat. Ahead, glued to Enzo, Céline was letting out little cries whenever the Tarantula gave them a jolt. Jo watched her sister, blurred by the speed: a year older, a birdbrain with the bearing of a queen. Sixteen years of thrashing in the world, glimpsing the abyss, blooming without maturing. Even prettier than the year before and a bit more stupid. Funny how it's Céline who's the eldest. Johanna isn't exactly responsible, but even at fifteen she has some of that desperate weariness that sometimes stands in for maturity.

Suddenly, Céline's head stopped bobbing about and fell onto Enzo's shoulder. But it didn't stay there, nestling like a girlfriend's: she fell backwards, shaken by the speed. Enzo panicked and tried to lift her to face him. He was holding the back of her neck as though it was about to break, shouting and waving his free arm like everyone else around. Jo

17

knew immediately that her sister had passed out, but she didn't scream. She waited for it to be over, for the spider to complete its crazy dance; just a few minutes to go, no more. Time always feels slower when you're perched up there but it would soon calm down, she knew it. Impossible to enjoy the dizziness at the moment. She was sure that idiot was going to be sick; it was written all over her face.

The cars slowed down and reached the ground. A kind of siren announced the end of the jolts; Enzo's cries finally alerted everybody and people flocked to get Céline out of the chrome-plated car. Sauveur cut the music – *at last*, Jo had time to tell herself – and rushed out of his booth. He had a good rant at everyone so they'd get out of the way, approached Céline and gave her a big slap, the first of many. Alerted by some kids, the parents ran over, along with Patrick and his wife. When the parents reached the ride, Céline finally sat up, opened her eyes, bent double and vomited at Enzo's feet. Jo's snigger marked the start of real trouble.

"What's wrong with her?" her father asked, his voice feeble and soaked in aniseed, vaguely worried.

Céline avoided her father's eye. She must have forbidden herself to think about it, pretending for many weeks, squashing her swollen breasts in a bra that was too tight. Unless she'd known from the start and pretended, as though it could just go away if you refused to believe it. But now she finally understood, when warm bile flowed up under her tongue like it had every day for a long time, and she wasn't the only one.

"Your daughter's not pregnant, is she?" Patrick's wife suddenly blurted out.

Horizons

"The first time, it's like a knitting needle piercing your insides," Céline had said.

"Then why do you do it?" Jo had asked, surprised, her mouth twisted in a grimace, clutching at her stomach over her belly button as though that's where it came in through.

She knew perfectly well where it came in through, it's not like she was stupid. But a knitting needle, that was a bit too graphic. She was thirteen, Céline fourteen.

"No, but afterwards it gets better."

It was two years ago, in "their" *borie*, that Céline explained why afterwards it got better. *Bories*, stone sheds in the south, are like bunkers on the beaches in the north, offering shelter beneath their stacked-up stones to clandestine smokers and secrets – and sometimes first fucks. And tramps.

"What's it like after?"

"Better, I told you. Weird, but quite nice."

She wrinkled her nose, smiling, her legs folded under her. The girls were slapping mosquitoes on their bare thighs. Jo's were also attractive, but that didn't particularly matter.

At just fourteen, Céline's triumphant breasts already heralded a bright future if she was able to use those charms. She soon started to attract the kind of appreciative, disrespectful looks from men that would get them a long way; in fact, she already belonged to these men. It took a while for her father to realize that Céline, true to the stereotype, knew without ever having learned. He'd been the first to praise her for it, proud as though she were a heifer, so he shouldn't have been surprised. Céline knew she was beautiful and took advantage of this, since she couldn't see anything beyond her talent for attracting men. As far as Céline was concerned, the horizon went as far as she could see. From her home, it took in the Luberon hills. From the windows of the technical lycée, she could push it as far as Mont Ventoux. Beyond that, her sister's horizon began. But that story was yet to come.

As soon as Jo comes in through the door, back from the lycée, her father is waiting, sitting at the kitchen table. They haven't mentioned it since the night of the fair; their eyes meet.

"Sit down."

She obeys without a word; she notices her mother's not there, nor is Céline.

"Did you know?"

"No."

"Don't treat me like a fucking idiot. I'll ask you again: who is it?"

He's covered in bits of concrete. His hands are almost white with it. Jo stares at the relief of tiny, solidified droplets. She latches onto the dotted patterns, gets lost in the flesh of his fingers. He clasps his glass. He's drunk already – a bit, not too much.

"I don't know, I swear."

"Don't swear. You must know."

Jo says no. She repeats it, shaking her head, lips sealed – and bores her odd eyes into his short-sighted gaze. He hates that. He loves his youngest but has always found her strange, and he's not the only one. Very soon, very early on, what with the silence and the odd eyes. One green, one blue, with similar undertones but no actual likeness. It was scary even when she was a kid. In any case it was too weird for people not to mind. Old people saw ill omens in her mismatched eyes, and her peers a strangeness which pigeonholed her in a different reality from theirs. Oddity has its advantages. Because they keep pretending not to see her in order to avoid looking into her eyes, people end up forgetting she's there. This encourages a certain quirkiness, and she sometimes takes advantage just so she can keep up her slightly mad act, this hazy screen between herself and others. Right now, with her father, she needs it. The truth is she really doesn't know who got her sister pregnant. She counts backwards three months, but can't think. It's hard to tell with her sister. The smooching behind the funfair rides was a long time ago. Céline is attractive, but let's not kid ourselves: for some people she's not much more than a tart.

"I don't know, really."

The father sighs. Jo is suddenly afraid he'll crack and break down. In his dark, aggressive face, the pale eyes are rimmed with eyelashes that are too long, like those of a child. The semi-darkness in the kitchen hides from Jo what she doesn't want to see. She'd rather have smacks – on the buttocks or across the face, it doesn't matter. But she doesn't want to see him bawling his eyes out. The clock is going *tick-tick-tick*, seconds turning with that stupid Mickey Mouse in the middle; she counts twelve before getting up. She opens the fridge, takes out two beers and puts one in front of her father. He looks up with gratitude and removes the top with his lighter. She lets him reach out for the second one. Then she goes out, with the second beer and a cigarette she took from his packet. She knows he's raised his head again and is looking at her through the plastic strip curtains. She can feel his eyes between her shoulder blades and on her behind.

"Where are you off to?"

It's not a threat, just a question.

She shrugs without answering and lights her cigarette. The lawn in the garden, already yellow from the summer, is rustling with insects. The bottle in her hand is still cool, but that won't last.

"I'll be back."

She runs to the scrubland to look for a shady spot, get away from the questions and drink her beer in solitude.

Taking Stock

In the silence of the kitchen, head pulled into his shoulders, the father is drinking his beer. Others will follow, since the night is young and he has things he wants to make hazy. Right now, everything is all too crystal clear in his head, clear and revolting, like that pretty daughter of his, legs open under the weight of a son of a bitch. And yet he knows that these days you're no virgin at sixteen. Or rarely. He knew it when he was the same age as his kid, and her mother wasn't much older. There were always some precious little madams who protected their virtue as if they were better than anybody else, or the ugly ones, or the dykes. But with Céline he should have known. Except that, shit, no, she was his kid. His first-born, his treasure, his pride. He took her to the jeweller himself – she must have been two – to get her little earlobes pierced. Tiny gold pendants to make her even prettier. Of course it wasn't always easy, and there'd often be slaps echoing in the house, but evidently he hadn't given her enough of them.

It had been tense on the building site that morning. He'd had a row with two guys in the team over nothing, some bloody nonsense because of a cement mixer. They'll hear about it, sooner or later. Not possible to make the baby go away any more, the stupid bitch has left it too late. And now she's a stupid bitch, like the mother said, and the mother's right. Yes, he should have been stricter, slaps are not enough, it's never enough with women. He can call her a *woman* now she is one, and she'll have a hard time of it. Patrick's worked it out, naturally. And he noticed the face he had on him, jaw clenched, mouth shut, chin tight like a snarl. When things got complicated with the other two builders, it was Patrick who calmed things down, he who generally flies off the handle.

Manuel has taken another beer. He's sweating. He should have a shower, wash off the sweat and the bits of concrete, but he can't, he can't be bothered to be new and clean. He'd rather stew in his own juice, his grime, keep turning it over and over, getting angrier. It's the time when even he doesn't know which way it'll swing: violence or snivelling, it depends.

His daughters, fifteen and sixteen. *His* daughters. Shit. Only yesterday he was the same age as they are now. All of a sudden, he starts thinking about his father, and that's not a good omen. And about his grandfather, of course. About the child he used to be, about old grudges. It's always the same with booze: you think you get away, but you end up slap in the middle of things even harder every time. Spain takes centre stage in the kitchen even though he's never set foot there. He gets up, stands still in front of the open fridge a few seconds for its coolness, and grabs another beer.

He didn't give a damn about Spain or that war everybody kept going on about. He wished it had never taken place. Moreover, he never wanted to learn the language, and that would drive his father crazy. But for fuck's sake, he was sick and tired of this condition they were dragging around like some glory: the splendid losers, living with history constantly in your face. Sick and tired of his grandfather and his dream of freedom dying under Franco's bullets. The stories about refugees in the concentration camp in Argèles. Shit! Nobody gave a damn about the war in Spain, especially not him. The others would pack girls onto gleaming scooters; even Patrick had got one for his fourteenth birthday, whereas he'd had to do up his dad's old moped, a wreck. He hated the residue of a Spanish accent in his voice even though he lived in France, and which would still tug at the end of his sentences, like a family song. And the revolutionary songs hollered on the way back from demonstrations. Sick and tired of being the grandson of a foreigner, and poor. And obliged to be proud of it. It was especially that which drove him crazy.

Still, at the Bastille Day dance, in Fontaine-de-Vaucluse, he managed to seduce Séverine. And managed to keep her, which was even harder. He was eighteen. Eighteen and his first apprentice wage in his pocket. His hair skilfully ruffled with gel – he wasn't shaving his head yet – and his arms already tanned from the building-site sun. Exit Spain, his father's trade union, the crappy apartment on the outskirts of Cavaillon. Exit the grandson of a refugee. Séverine was offering him her lips, and her breasts would be gently crushed against his chest as the Scorpions yelled *I'm still loving you*. He, too, would have his slice of the cake.

Manuel lifts his head and looks at the walls. His walls. Up to his neck in debt but the owner of his pasteboard house, his pink plaster house in the social-housing development built in the 1980s by a vaguely socialist town council. Except that he still owes his father-in-law so much cash that it doesn't really feel like it belongs to him. More like the house is his wife's. If he thinks about it a bit too much, he feels as though his balls have been cut off with a sickle. And now his daughter, as though he wasn't capable of taking care of her. He didn't write the rules of the game of life, either. The problem is that he used to think the opposite.

The Branches of the Paulownia

In the Arab living room, Céline is lying on the benches against the wall, like a recumbent effigy. Kadija speaks to her gently, offers her some tea. But she would have to sit up for that. "What did your mother say?"

"Nothing."

"What do you mean, nothing?"

"Nothing at all. She just wants to know who it is."

"And your father?"

Céline looks down. She doesn't want to talk about her father. Since he found out, she's been frightened of him. "He won't even talk to me any more. He acts like I don't exist then suddenly looks at me like he's never seen me before, like it's not me. Jo's the only one who isn't judging me. Not that you can ever tell what she's thinking…"

Saïd's mother strokes Céline's hair. She pushes her dark, dry fingers into the thick texture, rubbing the scalp. She shakes her head and makes little clicking sounds with her tongue. "Naturally. I want to know, too."

"What time is Saïd coming back?"

Kadija's silence makes Céline dodge the caresses and slowly sit up, her hands flat on the plastic cover of the bench. She looks at her intently and smiles broadly. "It's not Saïd, I swear."

"Glad to hear it."

Céline grows sullen, like a little girl.

"What's that supposed to mean?"

"My son needs a good girl."

"And you have no respect for me?"

Kadija fiddles with the teapot, takes the lid off and energetically crushes the leaves at the bottom with a spoon. "Look, Céline, I've seen you every day for sixteen years, I work for your grandfather and you've been playing with my son since kindergarten: you're like my own daughter…"

She goes no further, but there is a *but* hovering between them: resolute and irrevocable. Céline thinks about Sonia, who changes her clothes on the bus on her way to school, swaps her Decathlon sweatshirts for strapless tops, and wishes she could tell on her. Her mouth is burning with the urge to come out and say that she's fed up with the hypocrisy. That Kadija may not wear the veil on her head but she has one nice and thick over her eyes. She bites her lip. "In any case, Saïd doesn't give a shit about me, and he's not my type either, see."

Kadija sighs and assesses the damage to Céline's face. "It'll be all right. It always turns out all right in the end."

"You talking about my face or my life?"

The woman bursts into a velvety, warm, toothy laugh. "Both, my girl."

Céline grimaces and touches the bridge of her nose with her fingertips. Every morning, she goes through the same process to look good: powder, blusher, black eyeliner along the edge of the eyelashes. "You think I'll be attractive afterwards?"

"After what?"

"After my nose heals. I hope it won't stay crooked."

Kadija strokes Céline's belly with her eyes. "Is everything else OK?"

Céline frowns. It takes her a few seconds to understand. She looks down at her belly then rolls her eyes – it's all so over the top. A game of gestures, a constant comedy. "I have trouble zipping up my jeans, you know. I'm going to have to buy fatty sizes if this carries on."

Kadija watches as Céline writhes about trying to see her own bottom, then crosses her legs and smiles again. "You should go home, Céline. I'll tell Saïd to come and see you, if you like."

"But —"

"The children will be back soon, and I have to take care of them."

Céline sulks at being kicked out, however gently. For weeks now, she's been dragging her cute behind and her bruises to the neighbours' living room. Maybe partly to piss off her father, who doesn't like Arabs. But one thing's for sure: she's always sorry to have to go home. It stinks of reproach and shame there. Not to mention the fact that her father's slaps keep flying about. He crossed the line with his first thrashing. If he didn't kill her with his fists, his open hand across her face can't do her much harm. And when his mates come over for a drink, Céline disappears into her room. No showing off her slender thighs, her soft breasts or her slightly rounded belly. Her father doesn't like it.

"Get on with it," he always spits. "I'm sure you have something to do in your room, so don't embarrass me."

Her father's never been easy, but this is something else. You'd think she'd done it just to piss him off. He's suddenly looking ten years older, snarling like a pit bull, brow knitted over threatening eyes. So when she arrives home after Kadija's booted her out, and finds him chatting to Patrick, she hides behind her hair, pulls in her stomach and goes straight upstairs. The two men follow her with their eyes, saying nothing. Halfway up she stops, briefly looks at Patrick, then slices through the silence with a nervous voice: "Saïd's dropping by later."

She resumes climbing the stairs and shuts herself in her room. Headphones on, the music on max, she hugs her duvet the way you embrace a body or a security blanket. Céline rocks a little, with the light in her eyes. The heat's still stifling. She should have closed the shutters during the day, so the room would be cooler, but this morning she forgot. The paulownia branches reach out as far as her windows. She looks at the deep purple panicles, rotting already, stuck to the wood. It makes her feel a little queasy. She imagines they must be talking about her downstairs. Maybe calling her a tart. She turns up the sound even more, gets up and dances in front of the mirror. She sways her hips slowly: she's still OK face-on, but in profile she's already screwed; the inhabited bulge has transformed her figure. She's not going to cry.

Downstairs, Patrick shakes his head. He doesn't look at his friend, no doubt to avoid making him feel uncomfortable, and that's even worse. He stares at his beer, at his calloused fingers, the lemon-yellow sofa, the table legs, the porcelain ashtray, the picture on the sideboard: the one in which he's posing with his mate on the way back from a building site with Céline in his arms – she's four and a half, his large hard hat on her little head. He squints, sighs to make a sound in this oppressive silence, clenches his fists for good measure and presses them into his thighs as though they're about to start a fight there and then.

"Who's Saïd?"

"The neighbour. A childhood friend. Don't worry, it can't be him."

"Oh, really? And how can you be sure?"

"She's my daughter." The father has a little fit of pride. Don't push it.

"You can't trust a fucking Arab," Patrick adds.

"It's not him, I tell you."

"You gonna sit there and wait for the little bundle of joy to arrive so you can see who it looks like?"

The father sits up; his eyes are bloodshot. Lack of sleep and anger. "Actually, you're right. I don't know."

The poison acts, reaching deep into his brain. It soils everything and everybody, sticky like the giant paulownia leaves. Manuel pictures faces smashed by his fists, even hears the sound of cartilage breaking against his fingers. But the faces are blurred, many and nameless. He longs to fight – constantly and with everybody.

They've been working on a new building site for the past two days. It's a villa between Gordes and Bonnieux: an extension of the house, enlarging the pool, putting in a summer kitchen, a garden pond and an outbuilding for guests. The banal luxury of an area stuffed with idyllic enclaves, where there are as many private swimming pools as cicadas. All with stone cladding, naturally. Because, of course, they have taste. The owner says she didn't want it to take too long, you see, her daughter's getting married in August, so she'll have guests. With a little tinkling laugh, she went back into the house, with eight eloquent pairs of eyes glued to her buttocks. Not sure about the daughter, but they wouldn't have sneezed at the mother. *Rich bitch*, Manuel said through his teeth.

It just wouldn't go away. No. Fighting. All the time, with everybody.

Saïd picks this very moment to knock on the open door: "It's me. I've come to see Céline and Jo."

He comes through the plastic curtain and smiles at the two men sitting at the table. A red strip sticks to his hair. He pauses before the two men's look and their brutish body language.

"Clear off," the father grunts. "Céline's not here."

"What is it you want with her?" Patrick adds.

Saïd freezes and his smile turns into a grimace. He's eighteen and proud as a rooster, but his gut tells him the terrain is against him. He doesn't insist. "I'll come back later."

"No point. I don't want to see you hanging around my daughter, is that clear?"

The young man steps back even though the other two haven't moved from their chairs. He leaves without a word, while Céline's father yells once again so he can hear him from the street: "Did you hear that, you little shitface? Did you get that? I see you here again, you're dead!"

Fighting. All the time, with everybody.

Swimming Pools

It's something they've always done. At least since they've been old enough to slip out of the house without making a sound. Let loose like wild children in scrubland. Nobody's ever considered stopping them because nobody really knows. At night, every summer when the stifling heat begins, Jo and Céline sneak into the nice, still-empty properties to take advantage of their swimming pools. It's now become more of a ritual than a habit, and marks the start of the season. The Vaucluse is full of villas lived in one month a year, and they all have pools that are clean and lit from June onwards.

So when Jo grabbed two beach towels and got her sister out of bed, they didn't have to say anything. They've always shared a room, since the house isn't big enough for them to have one each. Even when their differences became obvious, clear even from the posters pinned to the walls, they had to adapt. They often declare their love for each other with slaps. And intimacy is a notion they acquired together.

They quietly slip over the windowsill and plunge into the night, climb over the short wall on the left and sprint without laughing until they're away from the neighbouring houses; they chuckle joyously once they're on the road. This summer will be different from the others, they know it – there's a menace in the heavy, already scorching air. They feel it in the pits of their stomachs but they carry on as though nothing's happening, as though the summer will keep its promises.

On the Chemin des Dames, they stop giggling and listen to the dry grass crackling under their feet. For their first bathe of the summer, they've chosen a villa they've known for a long time: it belongs to a slightly over-the-hill American actress who comes twice a year to bask in the sun with a lover. There's less surveillance than in politicians' houses. They sometimes have fun dodging this surveillance, playing cat and mouse with slumbering security men with thick glasses and walkie-talkies. Getting thrown out, running away half-naked, holding their flip-flops, running down the paths. Then, afterwards, talking about it, and laughing at the man's face, flabbergasted at finding two girls surface diving in a pool supposed to be smooth and empty until the owners arrive. They have some hysterical memories. But they don't feel like doing that tonight. Tonight, they're celebrating the beginning of the summer and the start of fucking problems, celebrating the end of something they can't quite give a name to. No point in adding any more thrills.

As they climb over the wire fencing Jo scrapes her hip, starts squealing and falls on the other side. Sitting on the grass, in the dark, she feels the tear in her shorts. Céline is nearby. She knows by the rustling of leaves and her stifled giggle. "You fucking stupid? It's not funny: I'm bleeding."

They silence the song of the frogs congregating in the stone basins. Jo stands up and forgets about the scratches from the metal and her torn shorts. They're extensive grounds, where you can weave through a hundred yards of truffle oaks to the beautiful blue pool without a ripple. They walk across familiar territory, even though they haven't been here for a long time. There are crackling sounds under their feet until the soft lawn takes them by surprise. Here, sprinklers make the grass greener; they can feel its sponginess under their sandals. They remove their shoes to feel the path, the soil beneath their bare soles.

Here they are: their reflection, their moving shadows defined on the villa walls, and the feeling of coolness that rises from the pool even before they've dived into it. At once familiar and thrilling. They tear off their clothes and jump in exactly at the same time, causing large eddies on the stone edge. Jo is the first to surface; she lies on her back and lets herself drift. Céline swims across the bottom of the pool, catches her breath on the other side and leans against the edge. They used to play at this being their own home, pretended they were princesses or starlets, chatted about a million crazy plans, about riding clubs and trips, putting on a posh accent. They stopped this game because Jo got fed up with it. For Jo, leaving is a real dream. Not necessarily to lead the life of a princess, but just to escape this one. She knows she's swimming illegally and uninvited in the pools of these rich people – and this always carries an illicit charm when all else fails.

Céline joins her sister in two powerful strokes. "What are we doing this summer?"

"I don't know. I'd like to earn some cash."

"Saïd's picking apples at Grandma and Grandad's."

"Yeah. I'd like a job too," Jo says.

"You?"

"Yeah, me. What's the matter with you?"

"What are you planning to do?"

"Patrick's cousin told me about a community bar in Avignon. It opens during the festival."

Jo lets herself sink. She hears Céline, Céline's laughter, and sounds stretching like an echo, but she can't make out the words. She stays like that a moment longer, her head numb under the water.

This is a game that began a long time ago; a secret game nobody, not even her sister, knows about: playing at drowning. Pretending to die. She stays underwater as long as possible, until her heart is thumping so hard it feels as though it's about to burst. She then shakes her head in every direction and it becomes weird: painful and pleasant at the same time. When she's on the edge, the very edge – or at least what she thinks is the very edge – she resurfaces and catches her breath, burning with the thought that she nearly died, and that she's in control of this unspeakable thing. Her first breath of air is amazing, absolutely brilliant. Her blood pulsating violently in her body as though it's about to split her veins, she feels the throbbing in her temples, her throat and her genitals, which suddenly swell up as though with desire. She loves that. Yes, she feels more alive than ever.

She comes back up, breathless. She didn't play the game to the very end because she's not alone. "What did you say?"

"I said you're not exactly stylish enough to be a waitress."

"It's a community bar, not a nightclub."

"And the difference is…?"

"Artists, actors go there, musicians. People who go to the theatre."

"In any case, you're not old enough. Besides, has Patrick's cousin seen your eyes?"

"Bitch."

"Does she know the customers are going to pretend they don't see you?"

"Shut the fuck up."

"If you work in the fields at Grandad's then at least the seasonal workers are so ugly they won't notice you're weird."

"I may be weird, but I don't screw everybody. And if I do, then I use a condom."

"You're the bitch."

Céline hurls herself at her sister and pushes down on her head with all her weight. Jo struggles, laughing hysterically before sinking, then grabs Céline by the waist and drags her down with her. They sink together. Their bodies get tangled up in a ballet slowed down by the water. Their heels hit the bottom of the pool and they dart back up and catch their breath, spluttering.

"Are you going to tell me who's the retard who screwed you this time? The guy who did this?"

Céline sticks out her lower lip as she chuckles, and accidentally gulps chlorinated water in the process.

"Who gives a shit?"

"What do you mean?"

"Who cares who it is? Even *I* don't care."

"You don't even know who it is?"

"Course I do."

"You're off your head."

"I know exactly who it is."

Jo gets the giggles. "Fuck, Céline…"

Their hiccuping laughter echoes against the stone walls of the villa. Their hair is stuck to their heads, their faces wet, their mouths open in a roaring laughter amplified by the night. Céline's black mascara is running under her eyes. Her belly and her breasts relax in the eddies. And the turquoise light of the swimming pool gives them a magnificent drowned glow.

They mustn't be too late. There's school in the morning.

Small Town

Sitting on the terrace of the Café de France, Séverine is waiting. She's on edge and that irritates her. Charlotte is coming, only Charlotte, so no point torturing her keys to the point of crushing the white rabbit hanging from the key ring. No point in checking her hair in her reflection and smoking four cigarettes only to crush them half-finished. Luckily, the owner of the café is ogling her, smiling, and she likes that; she's not twenty any more, so she must be grateful for what she can get.

Séverine did have her moment of glory, twenty years ago – *twenty*! She and her mate Sabrina had *it*, at the Privilège, the only nightclub in the region. It was so easy, with everyone's bodies so close. They existed in their flesh, electric – and played at being hard to get, while actually it wouldn't have taken much if they'd been handled differently. Just a little gentleness, a compliment, maybe some interest.

Their trick – hers and Sabrina's – was to dance glued to each other. Not exactly groundbreaking but as effective as the beginning of a porn film. Hair in their faces, shoulders bare, they would writhe under the lights every Saturday night. Séverine's parents allowed her. Youth had to have its way, after all. Her mother would sometimes worry about her getting home at night; it was about eighteen miles from the farm to the club, which was in an industrial district of Avignon. She'd always check what state the driver was in before letting Séverine go, but the driver is never drunk on the way there. They'd turn up at the farm, reeking of gel or perfume, with sparkling teeth and bracelets and a mouthful of polite *Good evening, Madame*s. She would let her daughter go. Her husband stayed in the background, as if this didn't really concern him. Sometimes, brutal and arbitrary, he'd make Séverine go and change if he thought she looked too sexy. But usually he was busy doing something else when she had to leave – counting crates of apples again, yelling at a worker or fixing the sulphate sprayer.

And yet there were problems sometimes. David and his cousin Jérémy had an accident one night, at the junction between the start of the main road to Marseilles and the access road to Cavaillon. The car had hit the barrier and ended up on the bank of the Rhône. It took the firefighters hours to get them out of there. After six months in a coma, David woke up a vegetable. For the last twenty years, he's been drooling, his face all skewed, wetting himself without even noticing. In the beginning his mother would take him out in a wheelchair but he'd start screaming, a heartbreaking sound, so she stopped. Now she just leaves him in front of the TV and he makes slobbering, grunting sounds of excitement at some of the programmes. The first few years, Jérémy would visit regularly. He'd been luckier: broken bones, but he'd recovered. He'd sit next to him, smoking a joint and talking to him a little, not much – stupid news snippets, like who was fucking who, or telling him about a funny film. The jokes would fall limply at his cousin's feet, which were turned inwards and tucked into sneakers that would never be anything but new. He'd stopped visiting because of his aunt, who couldn't stand to see him any more. Her eyes, full of reproach and distress – he was the one who had been at the wheel, blind drunk – drove him crazy. And actually it was a relief not to have to visit any more. Séverine remembers him going to work in Marseilles after that. She hasn't seen him for years, even though she was quite fond of him. Not as much as David, but he was all right.

When the boys would come to pick up Séverine – those old enough to drive – they'd turn down the stereo as they got onto the path leading up to the house. They'd also slow down, stifle their excitement, the urge to yell at the top of their voices that it was their turn tonight to try and hit the jackpot: to score with Séverine or Sabrina. Undress one of them on the back seat of the car. Just picturing it would fill them with unbridled, wild euphoria, and they'd be yelping like ferrets in the smoke-filled car. They'd agree beforehand which of the two would have which girl, as if it was in any way up to them. They had to calm down once the house was in sight, becoming *so-and-so's sons*, apologetic teenagers asking permission. Sometimes one of them would get his way, and the lucky winner would then talk about it for weeks, or just be content walking around with his arm around one of them, a proprietorial hand above her buttocks.

And then there was also Charlotte, who used to hang out with Séverine and Sabrina. The trio from hell. The boys had more trouble with Charlotte, who was too much hard work, and who'd arrived here halfway through her adolescence. To start with, she wasn't local, so it was obvious she couldn't always read their code. They didn't feel quite the lords of the manor with her, more like country bumpkins. Charlotte's parents weren't as lenient, so she had to climb over the wall to go with her friends. She was also more skittish, and even if the boys were ready to picture her naked in their arms, they weren't as willing to try their luck with her. The three girls were inseparable, smoking their cigarettes glamorously in the middle of the dance floor or coming out of school, laughing at everything, mocking like hyenas. Eventually, Charlotte had gone to study in Aix. And everything had changed.

"Have you been waiting long?"

"It's OK, not too long."

Charlotte plants three kisses on her old friend's cheeks and collapses into a chair with a sigh. Her sunglasses overwhelm her face but when she takes them off, the make-up under them is perfect. Not too little or too much, in good taste. It's because of this kind of detail that Séverine hates her. Bitch. *Perfect bitch.*

"You look amazing."

"Don't, I look like a vampire. Luckily, I'm staying with my parents for a few days, so I can recharge."

Recharge with what? Séverine wonders. She can't see anything except the green river Sorgue and the tourist-packed Sunday market. It's where she lives, not a Zen retreat. Recharge, my ass. Talking about asses, Charlotte's is still nice and firm and appreciated, judging from the owner, who affably makes a beeline for their table.

"What can I get you, girls?"

"White wine," Charlotte commands. "Two."

Séverine swallows, hating herself for saying nothing, but then who gives a shit? It's always been like this, so why would it change?

Charlotte decides, Charlotte lays down the law so naturally that there's no room to take offence or fight back. She's won from the outset. She often did before, but since she left it's got worse. You'd think she'd lose out on something, a point of reference or an advantage, but it's actually the opposite that's happened. She's got ahead while the other two have stayed here, stuck on repeat like the track on the Tarantula. Whenever Charlotte returns it's always as a tourist, always more or less single. For a time she lived with one of her university lecturers, then there were others, but they didn't stick around for long.

Séverine listens as Charlotte tells her about her latest love affair, some guy she met in a live music café and who dances like a god. Men here don't dance. They just stick to the bar and that's it. Or, if they do, then it's so they can rub themselves up against a woman rather than for the delight of moving, the solitary pleasure of a body spinning. That's for women. Charlotte goes back to her adolescent body language as she takes small sips of her white wine, pulls faces and rolls her eyes. After a while, Charlotte finally asks about Séverine, who raises her voice and laughs loudly as she emphasizes her domestic happiness. She talks about her job and says a few things about her daughters. She's not sure whether or not to mention Céline. Then Charlotte suddenly fixes her beautiful, perfectly made-up eyes on Séverine's, narrows them slightly and leans forward the way she used to when she was about to confess a truth or share a secret. Slowly, almost deliberately, she gently shakes her head and tousles her fringe with her fingertips. "I don't know how you do it: two teenage kids and twenty years with the same guy. Honestly, I couldn't handle it."

Something stirs inside Séverine, like a wave. Without letting go of her brilliantly untruthful smile, but with a slight tremor in her chesty laugh, she tells the bitch that she loves her life and wouldn't swap it for anything in the world.

"And," she concludes with a complicit little smile, "things with Manuel are as hot as they were at the beginning."

Charlotte shakes her head. Impervious – or not? – to the cruelty of her association of ideas, she carries on. "What about Sabrina? Any news?"

Sabrina, the last member of the amazing girl trio who reigned supreme in 1992, is currently vegetating in a Monclar high-rise. Not a penny in her pocket, with three children and three guys somewhere out there, she had to agree to move her family to whatever social housing she was allocated. Charlotte knows perfectly well that Sabrina spends her life writing letters of complaint, mad, paranoid letters, to the local authorities. That social services know her life by heart. That her attractive adolescent curves, which made boys salivate, turned into flab a long time ago, and that no guy wants to take her clothes off in the back of a car, or anywhere else for that matter.

"She's fine."

"Do you still see each other?"

"She lives too far away. With work and all... We don't meet up as often as we used to. Hardly ever, in fact."

Charlotte suddenly livens up, a girlish pout on her perfect face. "Remember the time Thierry was caught by his father after the party at Fred's house?"

Séverine tears the rabbit's head off her key ring. It was hanging on by a few threads. And now it's lying in the middle of the table like a bloodied trophy.

"I have to go."

"Really? So soon?"

"It was nice to see you."

They hug like before, smacking kisses, and Charlotte stays on the terrace with her book and her large sunglasses, like a Parisienne.

Séverine slowly walks away, trips over a flagstone, speeds

up, swears, then speeds up again. She clutches her bag. She keeps repeating that she won't see Charlotte again. She goes past the clothes shop she normally likes but hates right now. The entire collection suddenly looks totally boring. The sales assistant waves at her but Séverine cannot respond. She wishes she was living in a sprawling apartment complex, in a huge city where no sales assistant would remember her name, and nobody would know she's about to become a grandmother at thirty-four. A city that's not a village.

Back at the car, her chest heaves too hard with irregular breathing. Despite herself, she emits throaty little sounds, like a puppy that's being beaten. She drops her keys. She crouches, puts a hand on the asphalt, palm open, and lets out a deep breath. With her right hand, she fiddles with the little dolphin around her neck. Finally, she finds the rabbit's body and the keys, attached, and swoops them up with rage.

A gigantic city where she would not have grown up. A city where she would never have been twelve, or sixteen, or twenty. A city where she wouldn't have marked every bench and every wall with the insolence of her youth. When Séverine sits behind the wheel of her car, she doesn't start the engine straight away. She strokes the belly of the head-less rabbit for a long time, to calm herself down.

The Watershed

Saïd has parked his car in front of the Watershed. Leaning against the passenger door, he wipes his hands on his thighs once, twice, and again. They're clammy. He's not exactly afraid, but even so. He looks at the iron wheel, smooth with algae and moss, spinning in the river, slowly sinking against the current, coming back up filled with water. He checks the time on his mobile phone and puts it nervously into the back pocket of his jeans. He squints at the harsh morning light, and his stomach does a somersault every time a car drives through the dust. When Manuel's turns in, Saïd stiffens but does not panic. That's what he's here for, after all. The parking spaces aren't full yet: it's Sunday, second-hand market day in Isle-sur-la-Sorgue. Everybody parks in the city centre or in the surrounding areas. It's still quiet here. The Parisians will be along later to hang around by the river, have a drink and compare their supposed bargains. Saïd's hands are shaking. He puts them in his pockets. The ducks seem to be mocking him: there are ten or so chuckling and waddling about, and he feels like throwing rocks at them. Manuel parks at an angle in front of Saïd's car and turns off the ignition. By the time Manuel extricates himself from the pick-up truck, Saïd has put on his sunglasses and moved forward a little. They face each other at a respectable distance. They're the same height, except that Manuel is built like an ox and Saïd is as slender as a reed. He takes the lead – it's easier to talk than to tackle him in silence.

"Got anything for me?"

Manuel mutters something incomprehensible and gestures at the back of the pick-up with his arm. Saïd relaxes. He approaches the bed and lets Manuel slowly lift the tarpaulin.

"Odds and ends," the man announces.

Saïd rummages and finds a lamp. Copper and leather, old enough to impress an American. "I'll take this."

He continues looking, more sure of himself now. So the ritual clearly hasn't changed, despite the insults the other day. He concentrates so he can sort the wheat from the crappy, worthless chaff. Antique dealers have a good eye for this, and he's spent so much time with them he's learned the trick of ferreting out stuff that can be sold for an obscene price to the first Parisian or foreign tourist. He pushes away a rug that disintegrates, lifts the tarpaulin a little more, and discovers a section of a small, veneered secretaire. He lets out a whistle. "Not bad…"

"What about the rug?"

"You must be joking. It's threadbare; besides, this kind of thing isn't worth anything."

"Bloody hell, I busted my gut to bring it. It's fifteen feet by ten."

"OK, well, it's not worth anything. On the other hand, I'm taking the secretaire. And the lamp. Wait, let me look at the rest."

Saïd picks up a few art deco boxes and an enamelled bowl with a blue rim. He loads them into his car. Manuel doesn't lift a finger to help. "How much?" he asks.

The young man comes back and puts the lamp into the back of his car with the rest of the stuff, without answering. Manuel grabs the secretaire by the base and pulls it towards him. Saïd suddenly turns. "Careful, it's fragile!"

"How much?"

Saïd crosses his arms. He's still wearing his sunglasses and looks at his adversary from behind the dark lenses. He wants to stuff Manuel's insults down his throat and push his head into the metal wheel until he's swallowed so much mud he's crying and begging for mercy.

"Where's it from?"

"Same as usual."

Saïd shakes his head and gives a hint of a crafty smile. "You swiped the lamp and the trinkets from some old folk, or from some stiffs. Heirs don't give a shit and haven't got a clue about what's in Grandma and Grandad's attic – we both know that. It's easy to offload and we won't get any bother. Neither you nor me."

He pauses for the *you* and *me* together to sink into the builder's skull so that everything's crystal clear in his mind, fuzzy from stupidity and drink. *You* and *me* in the same boat, so if one falls into the water... "The secretaire, on the other hand..."

"What about the secretaire?"

"Where did it come from?"

Manuel's face clouds and he pushes the secretaire back under the tarpaulin. "If you don't want it —"

"Don't be stupid. I just want to be aware of the risks."

Manuel looks at the little shit putting on his act and also weighs the risks, all the risks. He hates this situation. "The same risk as the small painting last time."

"Well, at least now it's all clear."

"How much?"

Saïd sighs, faking embarrassment. He seems to think and hesitate. He takes out his wallet and hands him a five-hundred-euro note. Manuel frowns. "Is that all?"

"Hey, I'm the one taking the risk. Antique dealers don't like handling stolen goods. I mean ... they don't care if they're stolen from the dead, but if it's from rich people who are alive and kicking then it's immediately more complicated."

"While you're raking it in as the middleman, right?"

"I'm just a go-between, Manuel, you know that. And I'm an Arab, so if anything goes wrong then I'm always going to be the one who gets more flak than anybody else."

Manuel allows himself to laugh, a joyless laugh, tense with anger. "Don't expect me to feel sorry for you."

They help each other pull the secretaire out of the pick-up. Saïd collapses the back seats of his car and pushes other items away so the piece of furniture can slide in without being damaged. He spreads an old tartan blanket, covered in twigs and smelling of apples, over it.

Emboldened by the negotiation and cheered up by the advantageous deal, Saïd overplays his hand: "Our little business is doing well, Manuel, don't you agree?"

"Yeah," the other man mutters.

"We've been *doing deals* for six months mow, the two of us, and we've not fallen out..."

Manuel squints and sticks his chin out at the boy, waiting for what's next.

"Next time, think twice before you insult me."

"Are you threatening me? You're a kid, Saïd. I've known you since you pissed in your pants."

"I'm just saying: think twice. I'm not a snitch but don't piss me off too much either. Maybe your mate Patrick would be interested to know that you help yourself from the villas. Maybe he'd like a slice of the cake, too … just saying; I'm not saying anything."

"Then you'd better not say anything."

The builder turns around abruptly, gets behind the wheel of his pick-up and drives off. A flock of mallards scatters in front of the vehicle, which speeds up before disappearing behind the weeping willows.

Saïd stands motionless for a moment, dust in his eyes, slightly disappointed that no bird has ended up under the wheels.

He grabs his cigarettes from the glove compartment before locking the car. He heads briskly to the river, walks down three steps and sits on a stone, huffing and puffing as if he's just run the hundred-metre hurdles. The willow branches are dangling into the green stream. It's so quiet. Two branches of the river come together and merge, speed up into a waterfall that's wide rather than deep. A few hours from now, in addition to Parisians enjoying themselves, the riverbanks will be heaving with a bunch of kids in swimming trunks and sneakers who'll leap into the river, screaming. He was one of them not so long ago. With the same bunch of little morons and girls. Dozens of girls with golden or even dark skin. The ones he never dared chat up at high school and lost touch with when he became a seasonal worker and started all this wheeling and dealing. Other stuff was allowed here in the summer. You were strong and fearless; your courage was measured by the height of your leap and the audacity of your dive. The girls would jump out of the water, screaming it was freezing, their skin mottled, shivering in their towels. Some of them could dive as far as the boys while others would stay on the bank, feeling the cold, eyeballing them, sarcastic, assessing. It was for their benefit that the boys showed daring; after all, nobody was really interested in girls who were too brave. Except for Saïd. He remembered the slender bodies walking on the top of the waterfall, one foot in front of the other like on a tightrope, across the bank, all smooth and swaying their hips, arms spread out to keep their balance. The guys would be there drooling over their bottoms and the stretched fabric of their swimsuits. He used to drool too, especially when he thought about them afterwards.

You could play-fight in this water so you'd touch each other: catch a body and throw it in, sink, grab flesh with exquisite fervour, mess about and make-believe. Pretend anger and real slaps – thighs, shoulders, buttocks – the tiny sounds made by manhandled flesh, and insults: *You bastard, I can do that too! Go on, if you dare.* The giggling. Saïd would go and pick up Céline and Jo, they'd get into the car in swimsuits and flip-flops, sarongs tied at the back of their necks. He'd drive bare-chested, proud of the muscles clearly rippling under his skin – the incidental benefit of working in the fields. He'd still driven them back to the estate even as recently as last year.

Saïd turns back the clock and pictures the patterns on the swimsuits, year after year. Last year, Céline had a turquoise one with pearls between her breasts. Jo's was an old-fashioned dusky pink, a colour at odds with her angular body and incendiary aggressiveness. He suddenly feels old, too old for all that, and he's got better things to do right now than jumping into the Sorgue in football shorts and getting soft-skinned girls to scream by making waves and splashing. That makes him a little sad, with a sweet, almost pleasant sadness. He wonders if the sisters will come without him this year. Actually, he's not too old, no – he's just telling himself stories to feel more like a man.

When he lights his cigarette he notices his hands are still shaking, but he's rather pleased with himself when he sees the heap under the blanket through the tailgate. He knows an antique dealer who'll pay three times as much as what he gave Manuel to buy the secretaire off him. And who'll charge the first loaded tourist ten times as much: it's the law of the market, supply and demand.

Moby Dick

Waves of hot air rush in through the windows of the pick-up truck and mix with some crackling, at times slow-motion Led Zeppelin: the car radio still plays outmoded cassette tapes – the vehicle is almost as old as its driver. Manuel will be thirty-eight next autumn, but he feels like he's a thousand. Or twenty. A thousand from exhaustion, twenty from the rage. He tears down the road, northbound, in the opposite direction to his house, looking for somewhere anonymous to dump the rug. The green strip of fields as far as the eye can see does nothing to calm him down, nor do the cypress hedges. He wishes he could drive without needing to stop, eating up the miles while listening to his old idols, except he has to go back to the others at the building site. As a matter of fact, he should be there already. An hour late but five hundred in his pocket: not enough for his pride, but better than nothing.

He sees the grey containers on the side of the road, brakes abruptly and narrowly avoids being bumped by the car behind, which drives past with a blare of its horn. Manuel sticks a finger up at him through the open window and shouts a loud *Fuck you!* only he can hear. The tyres squeal violently and pebbles fly up against the radiator grille. Once the engine is off, the chords of "Moby Dick" reverberate inside the car: a friendly, almost heavy presence. The heat oppresses everything. Manuel wipes his forehead and the back of his neck with a dirty T-shirt lying on the passenger seat. He's so wound up he's feeling nauseous.

Taking the rug out of the pick-up truck takes less time than putting it in, but it's hard in the ruthless sun. The overpowering smell of the litter containers in summer stings his throat. Rotting fruit, mainly. It's true that the rug is crap, but how the hell does he know what's valuable and what's not? These stupid tourists are ready to pay a fortune for ugly old stuff he'd throw straight in the bin, so why not? Of course, if he had any money he wouldn't waste his time on this shit. The rug partly unrolls along the containers. Manuel holds on to the red-and-black interlacing and the string fringe for a moment, then gives it an angry kick and turns around. He sits behind the wheel and feels the seat moist from his own sweat. The wheel is scorching. For one thing, if he had any money, he'd get a new car. Maybe he'd keep this old rust bucket as a souvenir, since they've been through a lot together, nights in the open air in the back, him and Séverine. Some unforgettable nights, actually.

That was a long time ago. Back then, he'd put a mattress on the bodywork and she'd find it romantic to sleep there with him, in Saintes-Marie-de-la-Mer or even on the scrub-land, in those secret little spots only he knew. The indelible recollection of these trips is etched in his memory: Séverine liked to sweat and their clammy bodies to slide and stick. She liked this southern heat she'd never left, which burns even rocks. She liked the slap of flesh meeting flesh. A litre of water for every hour of lovemaking was the minimum. Afterwards Séverine would always get up to pee, and he can still hear her footsteps, the leap from the bed of the truck, the sound of leaves crushed by her bare feet, twigs snapping, and especially that of her urine spurting onto the ground a few feet away from the pick-up. A sound he's never forgotten, charged with excitement and tenderness. For Manuel, intimacy is that sound. That was a long time ago. Sometimes, looking up at the sky and squeezing his fingers, she'd say she wanted kids, many kids, but didn't specify if she wanted them with him. They were too young to know. And then the first pregnancy came much sooner than expected. Perhaps his little girl was conceived here, in the back of his pick-up truck. His eldest.

Manuel drives off quickly and makes a U-turn. He heads towards Bonnieux, thinking about his half-baked business, about Saïd, whom he was fond of when he was a kid – shit, kids should always stay kids. He thinks about his pregnant little girl, about the money he hasn't got or which he owes. About his father again; he must go and see him soon. And he remembers the nights of the past, when everything made sense and the future belonged to him. He thinks about it as though it's about someone else instead of him, and looks at what he has been.

The Way of the Cross

"What kind of career do you have in mind, Johanna?"

Jo shrugs, but without insolence. She forces a smile as she stares the careers adviser straight in the eye, hoping to make her feel uncomfortable. But it doesn't work with this one. Her two-tone look doesn't seem to bother the woman. Jo would quite like to leave, as it's the last day before the summer holidays, before she quits middle school for ever – is this really a good time to talk about this?

"You're very capable, you know, despite being a year behind."

Jo smiles. You're supposed to smile when you receive this kind of compliment. Gratitude and all that. It's true that she stuck out like a sore thumb among the other pupils this year, so it was time to quit. Too old, too mature, and harbouring that almost shocking brutality. She's never pissed anybody off, but none of the shitfaces carrying their Eastpaks in the school corridors would dare make the slightest remark to her. She spreads her legs under the table and pulls on her sleeveless T-shirt. Her breasts are so small she doesn't wear a bra. Her mother yells at her because of that, because it's indecent when your nipples stick out. As far as decency is concerned, there are far worse things that bug Jo. If guys – either pupils or teachers – want to ogle her 32A bosom, it's hardly going to rock her world or give her goosebumps. Jo's not Céline.

"Thanks."

"But you don't work hard enough. You've only had to repeat the year once, but I've seen your results: you always pull yourself together at the end of term. Clever, but it's a shame —"

"Yes, I know."

"You got involved in drama this year. That's good. I hope you carry on."

Jo doesn't reply.

The adviser lets out a staged little sigh. "And now you're going to the lycée. Very good. It's quite a feat, really, considering ... well..."

"What?"

"Let's just say that you do better than ... the rest of your family."

Jo rocks back and the chair legs creak dangerously. She slides into the woman's eyes, and without batting an eyelash attacks her with all her silent hostility. The adviser pretends not to see and continues. "But... Are you able to work at home? Is everything all right?"

"May I go now, Madame? I have to meet my sister."

The woman shakes her head and, resigned, indicates the door. "Go. Have a nice summer. And good luck at the lycée."

Jo sits at the side of the road outside the technical college, waiting for Céline. She's not afraid of the heat, and lets the sun hammer the back of her neck until it stings from sunburn. She scrapes the gravel on the asphalt with a small stick, creating tiny paths. Her tousled hair conceals her eyes and she blows it off her face; her bony shoulders stick out. Lycée pupils come out in clusters, and the sound of laughter and scooters fills the street. She raises her head and looks for her sister.

There's something hovering around her, a hollow sound in the wake of her former belle-of-the-ball aura. Whispers, embarrassed giggles, appalled silences. Eyes concentrate on Céline's belly then travel up to her pretty face, still a little damaged from the blows. There are many comments.

Jo watches the guard of dishonour, the fall. She feels pain on her sister's behalf but doesn't show it. Perfectly still, she takes in every movement of these animals, every yelp of the herd. And she follows with her eyes her sister's steps as she travels against the current for the first time in her life. Céline is almost walking in slow motion, slicing through the groups, lifting her chin to challenge the bitches who'd dare. Everybody stands aside to let her through, makes way so they can see her fall better. The rumour has become truth, confirmed by her silence.

Céline's mates push the kickstands with their sneakers and start their mopeds and scooters. Not one of them offers her a lift like they usually do; sometimes they even fight over the privilege, then one of the losers takes Jo home. They're always nice to Jo, as though they could score points with one by smiling at the other. Besides, they're a little scared of her. But today, the two-wheel dance takes another form. Embarrassed, they drive near Céline, turn around her, then one of them – perhaps Lucas – cuts her off, forcing her to stop. There are a few titters. He really wants an explanation. But Céline resumes the long walk across the street, towards her motionless sister. Another little guy, encouraged by the first, makes his scooter engine roar a little louder and brushes against Céline: she jumps. Her fright makes the sharks snigger. Céline stares at her sister's mop of hair and draws strength from her green eye. All she sees in it is steadiness, a presence that's always there. Neither judgement nor compassion. At a different time, Céline would have probably been the target for rotten fruit, pebbles and insults. The little witch who fell on her back too soon or too quickly. And who with?

Céline has finally crossed the road and looks at her sister from above, a hand on her hip to act cool. "Fuck, Jo, the nurse told social services. Dad's going to lose it again."

Jo doesn't reply, but rocks forward to get up. She darts a nasty look at the little shits who are making their mopeds roar. "Is the bastard who did this to you among this lot?"

"For fuck's sake, drop it, who gives a shit?"

Jo approaches Lucas, who's still sniggering, his face turned towards his mates. A kick in the shin and his cockiness comes crashing down clumsily. He clings to his handlebars like an idiot and the scooter tumbles down with him in slow motion, right in front of an audience without pity. His backside on the asphalt, he stammers in rage: "You fucking crazy?"

"Yeah, I'm crazy. And I can do a lot worse. It's not like you don't know me."

He can't think of an answer, grimacing with pain because of his shin – the bitch kicked him really hard.

"It's not as if you don't know my sister either, right?"

The teenager gets up and wipes his hands on his jeans. He knows everyone's looking at him. He can feel the audience's eyes burning the back of his neck with curiosity. She's a girl, so he can't hit her, the audience wouldn't like it: it would be in bad taste, a serious infringement of unspoken rules. But he really wishes he could, especially as he can't find the right words to wash away the insult and restore his advantage. And he wants to have the advantage, for the crowd to stay on his side, no matter how he does it. Between the laughing young man of the funfair and the aggressive one who stands opposite Jo, there's an abyss that smacks of crass stupidity.

"Yeah, I know her well. You, on the other hand, I'm not sure there'll ever be a guy who wants to fuck you."

Jo expected better than that; she smiles and, eyebrows arched with surprise, slowly whispers – to him alone, excluding the gaping mass – "Maybe you?"

She comes even closer, her face just a few inches from his, as though about to kiss or bite him. He's uncomfortable but doesn't want to step back – that would be too obvious a sign of weakness – but he hates this closeness and these odd, mocking eyes that are searching him. He's known her for a long time, but right here and now it's as if he's seeing her for the first time. Céline grabs Jo by the wrist and pulls her back. "Leave it, Jo. Let's go."

"You sure? Just as he was about to kiss me." She says it very loud, triggering a few giggles … the crowd could change sides. It makes Lucas's eyes fill with tears of rage. Small pink blotches appear on his face, a sign that he's panicking.

A car screeches to a stop next to them. Saïd flings open the door the way you draw a weapon.

"Come on," Céline insists. "Let's go."

Jo's smile broadens but she doesn't take her eyes off Lucas. The muscles in her slim arms are tense, her entire body braced for an attack. A smooth, dark animal with a dual gaze. Even Céline is sometimes frightened. But now it's Lucas weighing up the stakes, confused, hoping either she'll disappear or he will, anything as long as this face-to-face stand-off stops. He starts to blink and his leg starts throbbing with a light, needling pain. Jo slowly moves away, and he feels she knows something he doesn't, that she's seen through his weakness and won. "It's not me, anyway," he stutters.

"Get lost, you bastard."

In a slow movement, she finally turns to Saïd, who has approached without intervening. Lucas flinches at the insult but is no longer in a fit state to react. Moreover, Saïd's presence permits him to be less brave. Saïd has always protected the sisters, everyone knows that, so nobody would think of provoking him. And on top of that, he's an Arab, so for all they know he's got contacts among terrorists, you never can tell with all that's going on, so better be careful with them, he might be capable of blowing up the car for all they know.

Céline is already in the car, knees up, bare feet on the dashboard. Jo slumps in the back seat. With a sigh, Saïd starts the engine and lifts his sunglasses to wink at Jo in the rear-view mirror. "You scared him," he says.

"I hope so."

The small crowd behind them breaks up, starts to comment on the event and surrounds Lucas, who chases everybody away with an angry gesture.

The car speeds up, Saïd cuts across the roundabouts and the girls sway left and right, used to his driving. The car leaves the small town and takes the badly paved road that leads to the village: housing developments being built for the past ten years, a shopping centre, fields with apple trees. Jo drinks the poison of a landscape that's too familiar. Her nonchalance is just a facade; inside, there's a clash between love and revulsion for these paths travelled thousands of times.

"I'll drive you home, but I won't come in," Saïd says.

Céline tenses up. "I'm sorry."

"It's not your fault. I just don't feel like falling out with your father. Or if his mate Patrick starts rubbing me the wrong way, things could get messy."

Suddenly nauseous, Céline jumps and grabs the door handle. "Stop the car."

The wheels dig into the slope and Céline rushes out and bends over the grass, but nothing comes out. She takes big gulps of air, walks along the edge of the asphalt and shakes her hands down by her sides.

In the car, Jo slumps in the seat. "Oh, God, she does go on…"

"You're hard."

"Got a problem with that?"

"Pretend I said nothing. But you don't frighten me, cowboy."

He lifts the rim of an imaginary hat with his fingers pointed into a pistol. Jo consents to smile. Childhood always catches up with them – if it really is behind them and not hanging from their necks like a blood-engorged tick on a dog's back.

"Get on with it!" Jo shouts through the open window. "Puke, give birth, whatever, but hurry up. We're dying from the heat."

Céline shows her sister the middle finger and at the same time spits a string of bile into the ditch. She gathers her hair to one side so she doesn't dribble over it. Jo lies on the back seat so she can fully stretch. She cups her hands over her breasts through the sleeveless T-shirt and caresses the nipples with her thumbs, acting the prick-teaser, a role that doesn't become her and makes her gesture even more seductive. "Honestly, do you think they're too small?"

Saïd lights a joint without turning, takes two slow puffs, his face focused on the road; anyone would think he hadn't heard the question or was pretending not to if it weren't for a radiant smile that almost makes him handsome. That's when Céline comes back, sits down with a loud puff and slams the door shut. She smooths the sweaty hair stuck to her temples and apologizes, but no one pays attention.

Saïd turns around, a slightly gormless smile still on his face. Excluding Céline from the exchange, he hands Jo the joint. "Honestly? I think they're perfect."

Family

Manuel strokes the pattern on the melon peel. He follows the knobbly embossments with his fingertips, tries following a path, as though in a dream, then stops, picks up the fruit, feels its weight and rolls it in his large hand before putting it on the table and slicing it in two with a single blow of the knife. The sweet juice overflows and spills on the table. He splits it again and scrapes the contents of the middle cavity into a plate with the same knife. It makes his hands even stickier. "Nice colour."

His father-in-law does not answer. Of course it's a nice colour: it's his, his fruit, his land. Dark orange, sweet flesh. His melons aren't going to be anaemic, tasting of water, are they?

Manuel dreads these Sundays: family lunches at Séverine's parents', no way of avoiding the humiliation of duty, the reminder of his debt. Even during silences and exchanges with the others Manuel can sense the look of condemnation weighing over him, making him feel left out and wrapped in powerlessness. Perhaps he's imagining things – after all the old man doesn't say much – but he can see in his father-in-law's eyes a greyness tarnished by disappointment, a shadow that charges at Manuel. Not good enough. Not enterprising enough. A good-for-nothing who fucks his only daughter. A guy who smells of concrete, plaster and other people's houses. His father-in-law does get his hands dirty, though: he's not posh or intellectual. He likes action, expertise applied well. Still, he gets his hands in the soil less and less often, he has workers, and he's getting old. But it's his own land, it's not like building other people's houses and not being able to afford your own. They've had money problems too: the new regulations, expenses, falling prices … it's no picnic being a farmer, either. But as a good patriarch he was able to put something aside, worry day in, day out, so he wouldn't need anybody. Not him.

Besides, today is a special Sunday. On top of the usual unease, there's this huge piece of failure on the plates in front of them: Céline and her belly, Céline the unmarried mother – it's what they still call girls around these parts who are quick to jump into bed with just anybody. Séverine's mother has been tight-lipped since they got here, not said a word. But it's not her granddaughter she's looking at, neither at her nor the other one, or at her impossible revenge-craving son-in-law. She's watching her daughter, only her daughter, as though she's searching for something no one else can guess or speaking harsh words with her eyes. She goes from the dark indoors to the blindingly white light of the garden, carrying bottles and salad bowls. Her hands move briskly and abruptly, true to her manner. Séverine splendidly ignores her mother's look and her rushed agitation. She smokes a cigarette after every course and hangs around the kitchen only when her mother isn't there. A subtle dance, a fools' ballet.

Manuel drinks a little too quickly.

"They can work here this summer," the grandfather says, jutting his chin at Céline and Jo.

The former is pecking at pieces of melon on the tip of her knife. The latter is biting into them, her chin dripping with orange-coloured juice.

Around them, everything is screeching beneath the egg-yolk sun. The constant song of the cicadas is getting on their nerves, irritating their eardrums like tinnitus. The dog is dribbling in the dust, crushed by the heat, at the end of its chain. It's an old mastiff with droopy red eyelids and watery eyes. It suddenly lifts its head over a trifle, a sound only it can hear – a rodent, perhaps, or a very distant rifle shot: hunters are fond of this spot at all times of year. They're not in Corsica, but here, too, people like to make out they're stupid, bribe the *gendarmes* so they're more amenable, wear camouflage to find thrushes and rabbits, even out of hunting season. They never catch anything amazing – it's rare to get a deer, and besides, you'd get a hefty fine. The dog emits three snappy barks, its slobbering mouth turned up towards the table.

"Shut up!"

It's the grandfather who's shouted. The dog whimpers and lies down on its chain, its jaws slamming shut around nothing.

The grandmother turns to her granddaughters. "Johanna's too young. She's fifteen, so she can still go and bathe and enjoy the holidays. You can work with me, Céline. Not in the fields, of course, not in your state."

The first public mention. The rest has been said in the limbo of mobile phone communication from daughter to mother, reported orally to the husband between one thing and the other, one evening two weeks ago.

"I cook for the seasonal workers. You'll help me."

Céline puts out a wretched smile in reply to her grandmother. She hasn't got the choice, anyway. Things are closing in on her, but she has already worked here at the farm. She's helped out in the fields: cherries, melons and grape harvests at weekends, since those are in early autumn and you have to go to school, after all. But that was different. She realizes that something's changed, irremediably, and it makes her throat sting. She would also have liked to go bathing, loiter around the Cavaillon shopping centre, pinch lipsticks at Yves Rocher, ride on the back of scooters, run in the heat of the night. This is like a double punishment. Her grandmother's tone is one-sided, her suggestion brooks no refusal, and it's always been like that. Her grandmother has no gentleness. Like her daughter. Who knows if she ever had any in the past.

"I'd like to go to the festival," Jo suddenly announces.

Céline starts to breathe again, grateful to her sister for shifting the attention onto somebody else.

Her grandmother is surprised. "The Avignon Festival?"

"Yes."

"What do you want to go there for?"

All eyes, full of suspicion, turn on Jo. Céline wants to give her sister's knee a squeeze under the table for this extraordinary diversion; a wave of gratitude sweeps over her.

"They're doing a play I studied at school."

The faces relax slightly. Séverine tears strips from her cigarette packet.

"Theatre? You really want to go to the theatre?"

"Does the kid like theatre?" the old man asks.

Manuel really doesn't like this ever-growing feeling that he's losing his footing, that he understands things around him less and less. His wife, his daughters. He's not in control of anything any more. Theatre, and what next?

Séverine shakes her head. "Avignon's too far. I can't take you there, with my timetable."

"I'll take the bus. Or else I'll ask Saïd to drive me." She turns to her grandfather. "He'll have a few days off, won't he?"

"Who?"

"Saïd."

"Kadija's son? The Arab who never takes his Ray-Bans off?"

She nods without smiling.

"Do you hang around with him?"

The old man doesn't look pleased. Manuel is suddenly glad. Séverine gets annoyed. "The girls have been friends with him for sixteen years, Papa. They live just fifty yards down the road from us."

The grandfather scowls and helps himself to another glass of red. "Kadija's a hard worker."

Manuel pushes his glass forward so the old man fills it, but his father-in-law doesn't seem to notice. He bangs the bottle back down between the plates. Large wasps congregate at the bottom of the dishes or voraciously land inside melon peels.

"Moroccans are hard workers. In general."

"Oh really?" Manuel asks, tense and mocking, already drunk.

He grabs the bottle abandoned by the old man.

"They give you less crap than Algerians."

"That's for sure."

Manuel nods in agreement while pouring red wine into his glass – too quickly, so the wine splashes on his hand.

The grandfather doesn't join in. He doesn't like Arabs – who does, around here? – but today he refuses to side with his son-in-law in a clan agreement, a familiarity sanctioned by almost twenty years' worth of Sundays and the empty bottles of Ventoux strewn over the table. There's no getting away from the kid's pregnancy. You don't let that happen, not when you're a father. It's one thing if she sleeps around. But for God's sake make sure the son of a bitch who gets her pregnant marries her.

Manuel lifts his hand to his mouth and sucks the drops of wine running down his wrist. He's shrivelling inside. Inevitably, history repeats itself. And so does his rage, still restrained but insidious. The old man would almost say something good about that little shit Saïd just to piss him off, to rub it in that he's no better than an Arab.

Nothing's changed despite the camouflage, despite rejecting old family ways of thinking, despite Séverine and even despite the Arabs. Nothing's changed. Manuel is still poor. A poor idiot who reaps only contempt from his wife's father. Wheat that grows thanks to the soil. Of course, the landowner can act all superior. He has something tangible and living. And he doesn't even have to get his hands dirty any more. The blood of seasonal workers, the fruits of inheritance and an area bursting with sunlight. Ten ancestors in the local cemetery. Séverine is from here, but he never will be. He's landless and always will be. He'd hoped that the curse would stop at his daughters, that they'd be clever enough, like him, and marry local boys so that their children wouldn't be treated like foreigners.

He feels the old man's reproach acutely in his silence. The son of a bitch who got Séverine pregnant seventeen years ago, that was him. But if he'd refused to marry her, the old man would have got out his shotgun. The Spaniard's head would have exploded in flight like a pheasant hen, nobody has ever had the slightest doubt about that.

So hatred bubbles up again as well as suspicion, gnawing at him like woodworm.

His daughter, his darling daughter, so promising with her beauty – an even better version of her mother. He watches his eldest as she brushes hair away from her forehead. The question takes the shape of images and his rage rises another notch, picturing that bastard Saïd doing stuff to Céline. Picturing him turning him into a laughing stock by buying stolen goods from him for a pittance, then making a mint from those thieving antique dealers. Taking the piss out of him, yes. Having a laugh. *Bastard!* No, not a boy any more, but with wide, muscular shoulders, a man's shoulders. Making him the butt of his jokes. Making more money than him. Screwing his eldest daughter. The images take on the proportions of a nightmare in his head.

The afternoon settles in, heavy and yellow. Luckily, after coffee, the old man finally gets up and goes to have his nap, putting an end to the torture.

Manuel staggers a little as he approaches his pick-up truck, so Séverine snatches the keys from his hands before he has time to react.

"I'll drive. You've been drinking."

Not registering the deep hostility in Manuel's eyes, or his shaking hands, Séverine sits behind the wheel. She starts the engine as if running away, avoiding her mother's eyes. Manuel climbs into the passenger seat and sticks his elbow out of the window while his wife manoeuvres through the gravel. He's relieved that the old man doesn't see that he's not the one driving. He hasn't got the energy for a row, and Séverine can be tough, especially when her mother's nearby. The girls, slumped in the rear seat, slap each other so they can grab more space for themselves and stretch their legs until they start kicking each other with bare feet, children that they are. Manuel, too, wishes he could sleep now. Go home and sleep the whole afternoon. Let the rest of the world melt away in the already stifling, dense July heat. He doesn't want to think about anything – just sleep, sleep and silence the rising lava that's burning him like hell. He must go and see his father. But not today, no. He'll go later. He shuts his eyes.

Boredom

Johanna is walking under the sun. She was born of this heat, of sudden, slightly jerky lovemaking, on an evening of wine and clammy sleeplessness. She was born somewhat by chance, like Céline, but a year later. Her arrival into the world caused less of a stir than that of her sister: Séverine's youth was no longer as brazen, and anyway, her hip-swaying days at the Privilège were over. So another birth was in the natural order of things really. People even expected it to carry on – after all, the father was Spanish, so she was going to pop one out every year; Spaniards and Arabs, it was always the immigrants who were competing as to who'd produce more kids. The little girl's two-tone eyes weren't noticed at first. The doctor from the Mother and Baby Council didn't notice anything, and in any case he was more focused on the mother during the final check-up before the discharge from hospital, with a grimace halfway between dismay – second child and she's barely eighteen – and fascination: Séverine was still beautiful. It happened later, when she was about one: the blue iris turned grey-green; they said she must have seen something her childish eyes couldn't bear, they said it was a punishment, they said it was a magic eye that saw what others couldn't see; that her iris had turned inwards and that she had been changed by it. They said it was weird, that it was the omen of a future disaster. Here, anything even slightly unusual is commented on, dissected, and becomes a conversation topic. Through the lens of bar talk, self-righteous and drunk, there's no expedient apart from habit. Only habit can make something banal when it isn't.

But Johanna is grateful for this singularity. Maybe, she sometimes thinks, it's this strangeness that forces her to look elsewhere, to want to escape, to imagine worlds she doesn't yet know. Had she been lulled by the illusion of normality, she might have perhaps looked like her sister.

She bursts out laughing, here, right now, like a lunatic who gives herself permission to do so. There's no one to hear her, anyway. Immersed in the scrubland, she paces up and down looking for the rare shade of small pines sticky with sap, throws pebbles in front of her, and feels a little bored. She knows it well: here, boredom is an art form, almost a life art, and her own boredom stinks of anticipation. She doesn't feel like seeing her school friends or the village gang – she still hates Lucas and Enzo, the little shits she sees through with surprising clarity. Céline isn't here to add her own boredom to hers, and she misses that. They've spent their lives glued together for such a long time, despite their differences.

Jo is looking for ways out. She must be patient, but she has neither the age nor the temperament for patience. What she dreams of is explosions, magnificent events, nuclear wars. She is all pernicious expectation and anxiety. Céline's pregnancy doesn't actually change anything, and it's again about her sister, the centre of attention. But there's something hatching, buzzing in the thick atmosphere, in the family silences. She can feel it, like that sharp taste when biting into a green grape, on alert.

She breaks up the white stones and crouches to crumble them against other rocks. The light annihilates the slightest shady hole. Jo is envious of the tiniest creatures, the rustling insects. She dreams of setting fire to all this dryness so nothing will be left and the scorched earth will save itself by cracking open. And if the fire spreads as far as the villas and sets them alight, she wouldn't care if it also destroyed their house. She'll dance for joy on their mixed ashes.

Jo tumbles down a long, wild slope, scrapes her feet and ankles on the brambles and lands in a field of olive trees. She walks along a row of trees to the road and the houses where she lives. There's nothing to do here. Without two wheels, without a car, it's death. Even to go to Cavaillon – what for, anyway? – you need transport. She could have asked Saïd to drive her to the Watershed and they could have gone bathing. But facing a horde of bathers doesn't exactly turn her on. Actually, perhaps she feels better here, wandering around the countryside like an animal from the south, a lizard or something of the kind. The land still calms her outbursts, and, in spite of herself, anchors her to this area she so often hates. The land that extends its widespread power even despite her revulsion. Not the land she owns but the one that witnessed her birth and has trapped her like she's in a cradle.

She reaches the house via the road, clicking her flip-flops on the badly paved edge, her bare thighs warm and smooth like an otter's back, tanned by a relentless sun. The house is empty; she knows that and doesn't stop. She walks a little further. The door is open, so she goes into Saïd's house. She takes a while to find her bearings in the dark room; she's still blinded by the outside light. She finally makes out Saïd, leaning over a stack of fabric where a cat and a litter of kittens are lying. It's true that the black creature has been dragging herself around for weeks, fat as a pig, a swarm in her belly. The other day, Jo saw her come crashing down while trying to jump onto the wall enclosing the garden. She must have had her litter last night: the kittens are tiny. The young man looks up, smiles and motions to her to come closer. Jo takes two steps forward and freezes, her eyes glued to the basket. There's sudden nausea when she understands, revulsion at what's about to follow, but the disturbing lure of the scene forces her to look. She sits on the very edge of a gold-coloured seat.

When Saïd grabs one of the kittens in his large dark hands, the mother lifts her slitted eyes at the human she knows well, with a combination of total trust and pleading. The kitten he's just caught is whining in the palm of his hand. It's grey, a soft grey, almost blue, and its eyes, still blind, open and close, trying to grasp the world. Its pathetic cries reveal tiny little canines that are already sharp. Jo can almost hear its little animal heart beating against Saïd's fingers, its protruding ribs beneath the thin skin. She stands up and follows the young man, unable to take her eyes off that bundle of fur burning with life.

"You don't have to watch."

But she opens the bathroom door, lets him through and goes in after him.

At the bottom of the bath, three siblings of the little grey one are lying, limp, on a flannel: two black and one ginger. Jo steps back.

"Why are you looking if you find it disgusting?"

"I don't find it disgusting."

She kneels next to the bath, leans towards the little corpses and runs her fingers over their barely grown velvet coats. They're so small that she can only just get her thumb between their ears. She strokes a glossy black head and tells herself she could break the tiny skull if she pressed a little harder.

"What are you going to do with them afterwards?"

"What do you expect me to do? I'll throw them away."

Saïd presses ether-soaked cotton wool over the kitten's muzzle. The smell, like old hospitals, has permeated the bathroom. His bare upper torso dominates the space, his poser Ray-Bans are pushed up on his head. His skin is shining, sweat beading his arms. Jo gently bites the inside of her cheek; she can't bear the nauseating smell of the anaesthetic. "In with the rubbish?".

"Of course. Why, do you have a better idea?"

"I don't know. Can't you bury them?"

He looks at her in the mirror, his smile mocking, the dead kitten still in his hand. "You want them to have a little burial in a shoebox, with flowers?"

She gives a crooked smile at his teasing; she hates being caught red-handed committing sensitivity. "I just think it's disgusting throwing them away. With the heat and all, they'll rot and then stink."

Saïd gently puts the fourth kitten at the bottom of the bath. "I'm leaving her two of them. Sonia's giving a grey one to a friend, and my mother wants to keep one." He shrugs as he says this. "Nobody else wants to do this, you know."

In the smell of the ether, leaning over the dead kittens, their bare arms touch.

"Shall we do something else?" Saïd puts a hand on the girl's thigh as he speaks, and lets it travel inside, to the leg of her shorts that are too tight for him to go where he wants.

"Isn't your father here?"

"He went to the *bled* the day before yesterday. He's not coming back till August."

He slides a hand under her sleeveless T-shirt, over the warm skin of her stomach, and grabs a breast.

"What about your brother and sister?"

"He's taken Fouad and Nordine with him. Sonia's at a friend's."

"Who?"

"Sophie."

"That bitch?"

"Why do you say that?"

He brings his mouth to the nipple, erect in the middle of a tiny little breast. She gently pushes him away. "I don't like that."

Saïd teases. "Better not fuck you face-on."

He tries once again to glue his mouth to her breast.

"That depends."

He looks up and sees her smiling at him, revealing her beautiful teeth. She strokes his neck with her fingertips and pulls on the strap of her top to bare her shoulder. She's not quite sure what she wants, but when he slides his mouth down her stomach she stands up, having finally decided. "Shall we go to my place? There's no one in."

"If your father finds out —"

"Are you scared?"

"It's not that."

"Then what is it? Have you got an issue with my father I should know about?"

A brown lock falls aggressively over her blue eye. The green one challenges the young man.

"No, not at all. It's just that I'd rather not at your place…"

He senses that she's taken offence, so he looks at her for a few seconds without replying, a little wildly. Crap, he was nearly there. She pulls back her strap with a finger, moves away and gets up, a contemptuous pout on her lips. "No, you're right. It's so much better to feel each other up quickly in a shed that stinks of piss. Or shut up in a bathroom full of dead cats."

"Jo…"

She stands, slightly arched, one hand on the sink, the other on her hip. "Never mind. I'm off."

"No, wait."

He straightens up and tries to put his arms around her. She wrenches herself free, arm outstretched, hand open.

"Get off, you're pathetic."

Jo leaves the bathroom, gritting her teeth. He rushes after her. "Wait, please!"

"In your dreams! Touch yourself while thinking about my pussy. Next time, you'll be quicker off the mark."

She emerges into the light. People are small, the world without limits.

Coffee in an Algerian-Style Mug

Every morning, Séverine drops Céline off at her parents'. She never goes in. Sundays are more than enough. It's only just over a mile between their street and the grandparents' farmhouse, but Céline can't cycle while she's pregnant unless she wants to lose the child, which, after all, could be a solution. Except he might survive and be born deformed, or maybe an idiot. Nobody wants the same thing to happen to Céline as to the canteen manager's sister-in-law, the one who had a problem in her sixth month, now stuck with her daft kid, a backward face on a tortoise neck, all wrinkled and revolting. No school, goes to stay in a specialized centre for a bit of respite, but her life is over, finished, and her only occupation is her dribbling little monster who screams at every visit. So Séverine makes the detour on her way to work.

July is stretching out. Céline's pregnancy is very obvious now, as though acceptance has given her body permission to spread out. She's still kidding herself, but it's over: her belly has now placed her among the untouchables.

The old folks' property stands between a field of cherry trees and the vineyard. Nothing extraordinary, no swimming pool or grand verandahs or soft deckchairs. Stone and trees, muddy machines in the shed, earth-clotted tools standing against the west-facing wall. Austere, unchanged for years, since Séverine's childhood. A red tractor is parked beneath the branches of a huge linden tree. The other one, the one her father uses for sowing, isn't here. And the large table has pride of place under the window, the large table for family meals.

Séverine is feeling a strong wave of tiredness this morning, so when her mother motions to her to come in, she decides that, yes, it might be nice to be in her childhood kitchen with her mother and her daughter, drinking a coffee that's too white, in an Algerian-style pottery mug.

She parks her car under the linden tree, near the tractor. The farmworkers have already arrived, and are sitting here and there on the edge of the farmhouse. They're smoking, having a chat before work. There's about ten of them, in tank tops, mainly regulars, young ones and less young ones. A few women, all Arabs, including Kadija. Two students, no more. The old man has always favoured professionals. The old man isn't a natural-born teacher; and besides, he hates amateur kids: they can't understand how a team works, they adapt but don't grasp its complex harmonics and what's at stake in power relations. Like they give him dirty looks when he hauls a guy of sixty over the coals or checks the Gypsies' pockets whenever a tool is missing. Let them go back to their lecture halls and scrape scholarships to pay for their studio apartments. No way is his harvest going to be an exotic laboratory for shitty little intellectuals. He'd sooner have Arabs and Gypsies. There's a better understanding with them, even through hatred.

When Séverine and Céline walk past the workers, there's an outburst of greetings. The locals are glad to see Séverine, since they've known her for ever. But that's no reason for her to linger, although of course she responds, and there's a smacking of kisses. While Céline exchanges a few words with Saïd, Séverine gives a special smile to Pascal, who she's fond of, with who she went out in the fifth year, but with her daughter trailing behind her, her mother in the kitchen and work waiting, she doesn't feel like dragging her heels. Besides, she has no use for this little whirlwind of moments experienced a thousand times, departures and returns, family visits. Most of the time she just puts up with them, and sometimes tries – in vain – to ignore them.

They go into the house.

Céline kisses her grandmother. Séverine kisses her mother. All that barely touching with their lips. There's such a thing as reserve, after all.

Séverine's mother fills a flask of coffee and hands it to Céline, who takes it and turns back to serve coffee to the workers. Without looking at her daughter, the old woman washes her hands in the brown sandstone sink. She takes a long time to dry them. Séverine wonders why she has come in, why this stupid weakness, then remembers; she goes to get two Algerian-style mugs and puts them down on the oilcloth. She feels the slight softness under the canvas, the rubber tablecloth supposed to cushion blows and protect the varnished wood of a table that's too chunky. Séverine dreams of fine lines and glass tables, aware that even in her own home she hasn't been able to take on new tastes. She presses into the material with her fingertips, resisting the urge to dig her nails into it.

"Stop that," her mother hisses, as she pours the coffee and sits down opposite her daughter.

Laughter, livelier since Céline has joined the team, can be heard outside, along with Céline's voice.

"She's doing well. The girl knows how to go about it."

Since Séverine doesn't answer, the old woman adds, "She gets respect, don't kid yourself."

"I don't kid myself."

"You think you're better than her. You think you're better than everybody."

Séverine is suddenly overwhelmed with extreme tiredness, more extreme than the kind caused by lack of sleep, the lack of peace that sometimes afflicts her in the middle of the night. She looks up into her mother's eyes, pale blue and hard. She sighs. The old woman glances at the clock.

"What time do you start work?"

"Half an hour."

A silence, to estimate the small bundle of minutes, work out if there's enough time to spit out a few home truths, spoil the taste of the coffee.

"Let me remind you, you weren't much older."

"So? Did you jump for joy?"

"No."

"Were you proud? Were you happy?"

The old woman does not reply, her wrinkled smile frozen like a mask.

"It happened, that's all."

"It happened, so it might as well happen again, right?"

"There's nothing you can do about it now, can you? It's not like this child's going to swim back up into his father's balls."

Her eyes search Séverine, looking for an answer nobody has except Céline.

"We don't know who it is. She won't say. And you know something? Maybe she's right. Maybe he's not worth knowing."

"That's not the point," the old woman replies cuttingly.

"Then what *is* the point?"

"Dishonour, my girl. Tongues wagging, neighbours. The child, have you thought about the child?"

Séverine shakes her head, searching for help in a sip of coffee that's already lukewarm and revolting. Cheap coffee, always the same, because every little helps. And a rolling stone gathers no moss. And better a bird in the hand than two in the bush. And shit!

She downs the rest of the coffee from the pottery mug like a shot of vodka, throat open, elbow sticking out.

The old woman takes advantage. "Manuel married you, at least."

"Fuck, Maman, we're not talking about me, we're talking about Céline!"

"You'd better not use that tone with me, otherwise —"

"Otherwise what?"

"Otherwise I'll call your father."

She's walking – practically running – to the car when Pascal catches her by the arm. She frees herself with a violent jerk.

"Idiot! You scared me."

"It's only me."

"Well, give some kind of warning. You can't leap on people like that."

He smiles sheepishly. "I just wanted to know how you're doing."

"All right."

She opens the car door, dismissing him abruptly. The man pulls his head into his shoulders but cocks it to the side, smiling at an angle. He has the morning light in his eyes, making them look more bronze than brown. She remembers she used to be quite fond of him.

"I'm sorry."

"You're on edge. Is it your daughter?"

Behind Pascal, the workers are setting off to the field of apple trees.

"You should go. You know what my father's like."

"You know … there's quite a bit of talk about this…"

Séverine tenses up. Her face suddenly hardens, and the man can see her cheeks grow hollow as she tries to keep calm. He remembers her well from when they were teenagers, even though they weren't together for long. He would never have admitted it to his mates, but he was strangely in love, for a kid; so much so that he can remember details like this, like the soft skin in the crook of her elbows, and the smell of her hair and her sweat. Her cheeks, hollow with anger.

"It's just that… I don't know… I'd quite like to help you, you see."

"Help?"

"I mean to find the guy."

Séverine very gently shakes her head without looking away.

He realizes he's said something stupid.

"You're all the same."

"Séverine…"

"How's your wife?"

"Fine…"

"And your boy?"

"Fine."

"Good."

She gets into the car and slams the door. The noise of the engine drowns Pascal's last words and his pathetic attempt to say that he's not as stupid as she thinks.

The Path of the Drip

There's no one in the hospital corridors. It's the hottest part of the day and the patients are quietly dying in the muggy heat, with the fans on. Manuel moves forward like a dead man walking, his breath bubbling up thick and raucous, an echo of his father's, who is lying in the far room on the right. He can't remember the number but it doesn't matter, he knows where the room is, he could find it with his eyes shut, it's been a month now, and not long to go, the doctors said. He walks past the break room, the girls are laughing together, tired, their uniforms off, wearing sleeveless tops, slumped on plastic chairs, fiddling with cigarettes they'll smoke shortly when they drum up the courage to go downstairs. But it's too hot and their shift started so early. They look up at him and greet him with a smile. There's a bunch of photos pinned to the back wall: birth announcements, postcards with blondes embracing the camera lens on overexposed beaches. Right next to them are highlighted memos, roster lists, their individual timetables. One of the nurses fiddles with a packet of chocolate waffles, unbranded, mass-produced rubbish given out to the patients. The chocolate has melted inside the plastic, making them unappetizing. She stands up when she recognizes him.

"He'll be happy to see you."

Manuel grunts, nothing else. But he smiles at her anyway, because he's been taught to be charming with girls. This one's easily over fifty but as far as Manuel's concerned, even past a certain age women are still girls. Especially those you can touch, those who grew up not far from here or who do a job that gets their hands dirty.

She gives him an encouraging look. Unable to tell if he dreads it or hopes for it, she hears him murmur, "Is he asleep?"

The palliative care girls seem livelier than the others; it's something he's noticed while hanging around the hospital on his own, whenever he goes downstairs for a smoke or escapes his father's room to get a coffee from the machine. Something extra in their lipstick, bright, frequent laughter, a studied kindness when talking to close relatives. He sometimes wonders which of them will inform him. He can't remember their first names. It's the dark-haired one, the blonde, the one with the weird earrings, the fat one, the very young one. He can't tell the difference between nurses and carers. They form a vaguely reassuring magma, they do what he's incapable of doing: handle his father's broken, sick body, change his drip, spoon-feed him, wipe his backside. He doesn't want to think about it, but he looks at their hands, every time.

His soles stick to the linoleum, making a sucking sound with every step. A dirty sound. When he walks into the room he doesn't immediately look at the man who's lying there, but first follows the path of the drip. He knows this path and sees it even at night, especially at night, that and the pockmarked hand with thick veins, lying on the sheet like a dead animal, and the needle sticking into it. Then he goes up to the long face with its huge eyes and the head, almost smooth beneath the regrowth of fine hair – like the down of a duckling. The useless slippers at the foot of the bed, the air passing through his throat, his yellow fingers. Once again, Manuel makes an inventory, the route to the man who takes him back to his childhood by his mere presence. A few detours before daring to face his father and his end-of-the-world expression.

But today something is stirring beneath the sheet, the drip-free hand is moving up and down in the middle of the bed, lifting the sheet on and off. This breaks Manuel's train of thought and freezes him in an icy unease despite the heat.

"I can't any more," his father whispers, his eyes lost.

"Papa…"

"It doesn't come, even when the prettier ones wash me."

Manuel turns to the door, desperate to escape the embarrassment. "You'll see when it happens."

The hand emerges from under the sheet and, fragile, comes to rest beside the lying body.

The son is trembling inside, unpleasantly tense. He digs in his head to try and find an escape route. He looks at his father's hand. "You might lose it," Manuel says, indicating his father's wedding band.

The ring floats on his finger, now too thin, and sometimes slides to the joint.

"It won't go far, you know. Besides, I've never taken it off. I still think about your mother. Every day since she died."

"I know, Papa."

An artificial kind of silence occupies the space, filled with phlegmy breathing and ghosts. For God's sake, this window should be open wide in summer. Manuel leans on the bedpost, partly because he feels nauseous but mainly because he can't think of what to say. At the same time it's nothing new, things were actually worse before. But now that death is imminent there's stuff coming up, said straight out without respecting boundaries, conventions forgotten, and he doesn't like that. It hurts him to see the old man so diminished, even though he's dreamed of confronting him a thousand times. Especially as he's dreamed of confronting him a thousand times. It drives him crazy, this illness, the tubes, the end. When will it stop, for crying out loud? he thinks. And his shame at thinking that so intently eats away at him.

"How's Séverine?"

"Fine."

"She has a difficult job. All these kids, it's good what she does."

"She's a lunchtime supervisor, Papa. She just serves them food, that's all."

"You think feeding kids is nothing?"

"Papa…"

The old man runs out of breath, and Manuel gets frightened. He's sorry once again. "Did I tell you I'm working on a site in Bonnieux? We're rebuilding a drystone wall, it was quite tricky, I wish you could have seen it."

His father's large eyes get lost on the window frame. "Tell the girls to come and see me."

"… The boss said it looks good, so maybe next time round he'll put me in charge of the team."

"It's not long now and they're on holiday, so they can come."

A new silence, worse than the previous one, marks the end of the visit.

There are magazines lying on the night table – *La Marseillaise, La Provence* – that are several days old. Manuel wonders who brings them to him. A nurse, perhaps. Or

Séverine, who sometimes stops by to give his father a kiss on her way back from work. He forces a smile before leaving the room, and turns one more time to look at his father.

"I'll tell them, Papa."

Edward Bond

"That was brilliant!"

The girl says it with the grave face of eternal faith. Jo clings to this fervour she's just shared for forty minutes in the tiny Bourg-Neuf Theatre. There aren't many of them here for the performance of Edward Bond's *Summer*: five audience members, but the guy at the door said *We'll play anyway, it's Avignon, it's like that, there are too many theatres and too many shows, so five people in the audience isn't too bad.* He was wearing make-up, he was also acting in the play – and no doubt doing the driving, acting, taking the set down and doing the cleaning. The city is saturated with posters and people, too many, of course, a strange madness that's a bit tackier every year. The Avignon Festival has taken on new identities. In the past, there was that magical excitement, the square in front of the Palais des Papes covered in magnificent savages, with or without costumes, acting or braiding long hair, reciting poetry even to the stones beneath their feet, sublime beggars. At night, parties and acrobatic, drunken climbing of the slopes of the Rocher des Doms despite municipal prohibition. They still have parties in the secluded enclosures of the palace court-yard and theatre back rooms, but between prohibitions and decrees, and increasingly right-wing social cleansing, every year Avignon looks more and more like a set, a *Truman Show* to which Parisians and tourists flock during the festival. Everybody agrees that the festival is even better than before.

It's all very new to Johanna, so she obviously finds these thousands of posters devouring the walls in the city and these people who've come from other places very exciting. Moreover, she's particularly fascinated by the processions. She's bowled over by the actors parading in the middle of the street, in full costume and yelling out lines, haranguing crowds sitting outside cafés. In her world everybody tries to hold on to their haughtiness, however pathetic. At school, naturally, but not only there. Her father would never agree to go to a fancy dress party, he'd feel totally humiliated. Seeing some people adopt grimaces, make-up and *the game* opens new horizons before her. She feels uncomfortable but her boundaries shift, and the sense of ridicule switches sides.

The girl smiles at her. "The direction was excellent. Did you enjoy it?"

Jo wonders if she's from Paris. Her politeness is studied, over the top and a bit condescending. Enraptured like a nun in ecstasy but her every gesture abiding by a code of elegance that makes Jo feel ugly, poor and stupid.

"Yes."

"And there's such a perception, such an understanding of the script – I love this play. Bond is truly unique."

Jo nods. She'd never heard of Bond until today. Her drama teacher at school vaguely tried to make them act out a few extracts from Molière. "Yes, it was great."

She really thinks it. She also found it moving, even though she lacks the words to express it. She wishes she had them, right here and now, so she can respond to this incredible girl, not much older than her, who seems so sure of herself. Jo wants to hit her, become her best friend, or be her, it's impossible to tell which. She picked this play because she liked the poster, because the tickets weren't expensive – an advantage of the festival, the undercutting among companies competing for survival. Her phone rings. Saïd. The girl keeps staring at her, and doesn't look like she wants to leave. She seems to find Jo's company interesting. Jo moves away a little to answer Saïd. *No, not yet, but yes, come and pick me up. What? Not now, but in a little while. I know you're coming especially! In half an hour, by the ramparts at Porte Sainte-Catherine.*

She turns to the girl, puts the phone in her pocket with a guilty expression as if the girl could see what Saïd looks like, his crummy car, and even hear his accent. The girl doesn't have one. They walk to Rue des Teinturiers together. She talks about some wonderful play or other she's read, does Johanna know it? Her name's Garance. Jo has a bit of a tummy ache; she doesn't know what to say and hates the fact that this bothers her. She wants not to give a shit about it, like she usually doesn't give a shit about posh people. But the bitches at her school who go horse-riding on Wednesday afternoons haven't read Edward Bond. She suddenly feels this vague sense of unease, the divide that shows that money opens the doors to a world besides the one with expensive cars and holidays abroad. It's not the first time but it suddenly takes shape, in the words of this girl, the passion that mirrors hers but is much better nurtured. Johanna feels betrayed.

"Do you live here?"

Garance nods. "My mother lives within the city walls. I go to the Lycée Saint-Joseph."

"Of course you do," Jo blurts out, sniggering.

"Yeah, I know," Garance says, squinting at her, taking the sarcasm on the chin. But perhaps she's also slightly embarrassed.

"Sorry…"

"Don't worry about it, I get it. But it's really not that bad, you know."

Jo doesn't answer.

The street, cluttered with tables, makes Jo want to stop here and spend hours drinking ice-cold Coke. Garance suddenly sees some friends of hers and starts emitting joyful little screams as she calls out to them. Sitting around a table planted in sand – a trendy café that provides the illusion of a beach in the very heart of Avignon – Garance's friends respond with equally over-the-top, euphoric shrieks. This really annoys Jo. She doesn't say hello, keeps her hands deep in her pockets and looks the table up and down without warmth. She thinks they're attractive and brilliant. Her stomach cramps really hurt and she doesn't like the situation, these people who scream hysterically when they say hello. A bit like Céline and her friends, but not exactly the same, either.

"Will you have a drink with us?" Garance suggests.

"No, I can't."

"It's on me."

"It's OK, I've got the cash, I don't need you to pay for me."

"That's not what I meant."

Jo fixes her two odd eyes on the other girl's, and the latter lights up with a smile.

"You've got amazing eyes, gosh, I hadn't noticed before."

All of a sudden it's Jo who feels sick; shit, it's not every day she gets a compliment. She can tell perfectly well it's not flirting, and it's not poking fun, either. Jo bites her lip and looks around her as if she expects to find a parade in honour of embarrassment. But it's Garance who settles the argument, totally unaware of anything. "Give me your number. I'll call you, then you'll have mine."

Garance's mates have resumed their conversation, talking about music. Jo's never understood how you can talk about music. Music isn't about talking, it's about listening. At most you can dance to it or get someone else to listen to it – just about.

"What for?"

"We're having a party in Gordes in a couple of weeks, at my father's house, a huge affair to celebrate the end of the festival. With some friends. Do you want to come?"

Jo shrugs, looking as if she couldn't care less. She's dying to go to this party.

She gives Garance her number.

Never Be Like Them

The guys finished early and didn't linger at the bookie's. They quite like to do that, as a habit, but lately Manuel has been short on diplomacy so Patrick suggested a drink somewhere else: he didn't want his mate to lose it and smash another worker's face.

Usually, it's the other way around: Patrick is as prickly as a horsefly, ready to scrape his knuckles on the jaw of the first man who contradicts him, just for the atavistic pleasure of a fist fight. Manuel calms things down when he can, smooths any sharp corners with friendly words and conciliatory beers. Once, only once, did he take a punch, but it wasn't aimed at him; just an error in calculation, the target was moving too much and Manuel too intent on preventing the fight. It calmed everyone down. Because Manuel was the strongest, everyone knew that. You just had to see the size of the stones he lifted when building a wall. You just had to see the speed at which he could build one. And the size of his calloused hands. Nobody fucked with him if they didn't want to be flattened by a blow as powerful as a boxer's punch. Every muscle bulged like a threat, a challenge to the rest of the gang.

They arrive at Manuel's with packs of beer in each hand, bare-chested, their T-shirts tucked into the belts of their trousers, slapping the backs of their thighs like animal tails. Séverine is watching television on the sofa.

"Should have told me you weren't coming back home alone, would have dolled myself up a bit."

Patrick laughs, plants a kiss on Séverine's temple; she barely lifts her head so she doesn't miss a detail of her programme – girls dancing on a stage and then getting insulted by their coach. One of them is crying in her dressing room and you can see her sniffing in close-up, lipstick spread over her wet cheek.

Over the years, Patrick has seen her dressed even worse, so a pair of leggings and a sleeveless top aren't exactly going to give him a heart attack.

"Where's Valérie?" Séverine asks.

"At home, but she'll join us, if that's OK."

"Of course she can come for a drink; I've also got some leftovers."

A beer in his hand, Manuel comes to stand right in the middle of the living room. "We have to be up early tomorrow."

Patrick is in the process of texting his wife to tell her to join them. "Don't worry, we're not about to camp here all night…"

Séverine rolls her eyes, creating a complicity with Patrick against her husband, such a square. "Did you buy the beer just for yourself?"

"Be my guest."

Patrick sniggers and goes to fetch two beers, one for himself and one for the wife of his mate, the great lord. Picking off bits of silicone stuck to his fingers, Manuel asks if the girls are back.

"Céline's in her room."

"What about Jo?"

"Not yet. She's hanging around with a new friend and spends her time in Avignon."

"A new friend?" Patrick, who's known the girls since before they existed, asks.

Séverine turns her head towards him – the dancers on the screen are tackling a routine, dressed like Texan whores. "Yeah, a new friend who goes to the Lycée Saint-Joseph."

The two of them snigger. Not Manuel. "You find that funny?"

"Well, yeah. What's with you and the long face? Can't we relax a little?"

"I'd also send the child to Saint-Joseph, if I could."

"Stop that bullshit. She'll do very well at Cavaillon," Séverine says sharply.

"So she ends up like her sister?"

"I don't see the connection," Séverine replies, more harshly.

"You don't?"

"You think posh girls don't get knocked up?"

Patrick goes to the door while drinking his beer. He pretends to be looking out for Valérie and walks through the plastic curtain as if on his way to meet her. In actual fact, he strolls a few feet and looks at the Luberon river, which is turning orange at this time of day. But he can still hear their voices.

"I don't know, perhaps they realize it sooner."

"Can we just not talk about it for one evening? Do you think that's possible?"

Patrick lights a cigarette with his Zippo. He finds the familiar smell of petrol reassuring. He clenches his jaw and bites the filter. Séverine must have turned up the volume because a reprise of "Jolene" now invades the garden. The singer's voice has nothing of Dolly Parton's biting despair, but her *please don't take him just because you can* still makes

Patrick quiver. He glances up at the open window of the girls' room. Céline is leaning on the sill, in a bra, smoking a joint. She looks at him without saying anything, takes a drag from the carton filter slowly, so she doesn't burn herself. They remain like this for a moment. He can't see her belly, below, just her breasts overflowing, the lace on the edge of her cleavage, the soft, puffy flesh. And her expressionless eyes that don't let go of his. He remembers the day Manuel turned up at the bookie's like a maniac to announce her birth, his hands shaking, his eyes moist like a girl's. And the bender that followed. He wonders what she's thinking about, and his heart is beating too fast. She throws down the still-smouldering butt and it lands at his feet. He crushes it with the tip of his shoe. Then he looks up again, but Céline has disappeared.

Finally, it's Manuel and Séverine who come and join Patrick in the garden. Séverine has put on a T-shirt and skirt and tied her hair in a ponytail like an American cheerleader with a few extra miles. But she carries them well. When Valérie turns up, she brings peanuts; a huge pack of monkey nuts goes well with beer. Then the men move on to pastis. They talk about the building site, about Bonnieux and the ornamental pond the owner is making them dig right next to the pool. They talk with a mixture of envy and mockery, because an ornamental pond is pointless, it's crazy, a rich woman's whim.

"But what's it for?" Valérie insists.

"It's just pretty. Or else to put fish in it, don't know."

Patrick sniggers. He crushes the peanut shells between his fingers, takes out the nuts, and crunches them two by two. A heap of stringy shells piles up in the ashtray, about to spill over. Every so often he gives the window a furtive glance, looking out despite himself for Céline's outline, although she doesn't reappear. Manuel tries to present a calmer face to his wife, his mate and his mate's wife. He tells himself that Séverine is prettier than Valérie and her extra kilos, blonde hair cut across her forehead and cheap drop earrings. It's a pleasant thought. He tells himself it feels good to be here, at the end of a working day – he almost convinces himself. He banishes his father, he banishes his daughter. He drinks a little too quickly.

You can still hear the TV through the open doors and windows, snippets of dreadful and spectacular news which, at first sight, don't seem to concern the masses. Bombs have razed several villages in the Middle East to the ground; some shareholders have collected millions of euros' worth of dividends; some trade unionists are trying to reach an agreement with the owners of a large company to avoid two thousand redundancies.

"Should let them all die," Manuel says.

"Or make them live on the minimum wage," Valérie suggests. Valérie's sweet. Well, not always, but she still has a teacher's tendency, a stand against violence, even though she's the first to get it smack in the face. Everybody knows. Everybody keeps quiet about it because it doesn't happen very often, Patrick's not a bad sort, and life isn't easy for anybody. Besides, when she starts, when things start sizzling between them, it's not like she just stands there with her arms crossed.

The news carries on: a mother has found her daughter after an absence of twenty years. An old singer is dead. A radicalized cell on the outskirts of Paris has been dismantled.

A refugee camp has been set fire to in the east. The state of emergency has been extended.

The noise of an engine suddenly drowns out the news and a car slowly drives into the compound, an unfamiliar car. Here, everybody knows everybody else's car, the make and production date, even the stickers on the back, the *Baby on Board* and the *Go On, Overtake Me, You Bastard*. No one's ever seen this one, a new Audi A3, black as ink, that slows down and stops outside the house. Dark windows, so impossible to see the driver. The drinkers fall silent. Jo's legs emerge from the passenger seat. She jumps out of the car, her hair still wet, a childlike expression in her smile, and shuts the door behind her. To greet her parents and the others she resumes a joyless mask, and plants kisses on their cheeks as though it's an ordeal. The four adults are still quiet. And yet everyone wants to know.

The car starts again and slowly goes to park fifty yards further down the street. Around the table, the silence persists, heavy with questions. The wall is low enough for everybody to spy on their neighbours; the four of them twist their necks to see the car and its occupant. Saïd gets out. He locks the car with his key; it makes a noise like a light sabre and the headlights blink before going out. He goes into his house.

"What's that car?" Manuel finally grumbles.

"The little shit has money," Patrick hisses.

Jo shakes her head. "Well, he works."

"To afford a car like that with a job as a seasonal worker…"

Manuel doesn't say anything. He stares, his blind man's eyes turned inwards.

"Pour me some more pastis," he tells Séverine, and she complies without whining.

There are moments like this when she understands. Quite often, in fact, though she doesn't let on. Sometimes, she just pretends she doesn't get it. She looks at her daughter standing in the falling darkness, hesitating between sitting down and going upstairs to her sister.

"What did you do today?"

"Nothing."

"Nothing?"

"I saw a play in Avignon, then went for a swim in the Sorgue."

"Was it nice?"

"All right." Jo shrugs and grabs a handful of peanuts.

"Is it monkeys you feed peanuts?" Patrick asks.

"You're the monkey!" Patrick gives her a slap on the thigh; she pulls away and gives him an icy look. He doesn't give a damn and starts mimicking a chimpanzee, emitting stupid cries. She suddenly smiles, despite herself.

"Bye, oldies," she says before going into the house.

"I'm not hungry."

"Make a little effort."

The frozen pizza Jo has cooked in the microwave gives off a smell of fat and Herbes de Provence.

"It's too hot to eat stuff like that."

"Come on…"

"It makes me want to puke."

"I thought you were feeling better."

"Yeah, but if you stick that under my nose I might throw up again."

Jo nibbles at her pizza slice, slumped on her bed, opposite Céline's. "Is it going OK with Grandma? Are you coping?"

"Yeah."

Céline puts a hand on her naked, round belly. With her pink fingernails she picks at her navel, strokes the skin around it in a spiral movement, expanding the circle then returning to the middle. "Are Patrick and Valérie still here?"

"Can't you hear them?"

Bursts of laughter, advice on everything and fragments of jokes rise to the bedroom. Valérie laughs too loudly.

"Yes."

Céline sighs as if she's dying, an arm over her face, her closed eyes still made up.

"Did you go to the river with Saïd? I didn't see him at work today."

"Yeah."

"Oh great, you're a real laugh, you don't spare any details, it feels like you're sharing, it's really nice."

Jo laughs silently. "I saw my mate again, the one in Avignon."

"Do tell."

"We went to see some plays."

"Oh, what a bundle of laughs…"

"There's a party at her house in two weeks' time. Want to come?"

Céline rolls on her side, a fist stuck into her cheek. "I'm spending the summer at our grandparents' among all the grubby lot and don't see anybody. So, yes, I'd like to come to your fancy party. Anything to escape this fucking shitty summer." She leans down to pick up a piece of pizza. The cheese has hardened. It looks revolting but her sister's right, she should have something. They eat in silence, hoping in vain for a breath of air to come through the window. But the night is still muggy. Their father's voice rises up to them but they can't make out the words.

"Jo?"

"Yes?"

"We'll never be like them, right?"

Jo doesn't answer straight away. She hesitates and considers the appropriateness of too direct a reply. In her doubt, she opts for a half-lie. "No, never."

"Manuel, you stink."

"Séverine…"

"You didn't even have a shower when you got home." She grits her teeth and her eyes drift beyond the man who's rubbing himself against her, breathing too heavily. "Get off me."

Patrick and Valérie left after the peanuts and beer. The girls didn't come back out of their room and won't before tomorrow. So they ate the leftover chicken on the sofa and watched the end of a crappy film, a romantic comedy with a highly predictable outcome. Without talking, without bringing up painful subjects – respite.

Then Séverine got up to put the plates in the dishwasher. Manuel followed her legs and her backside, excited all of a sudden.

"Stop it, not now."

He tries to kiss her, presses himself against her, presses her against the wall, she usually likes that, when he's stronger than her. She used to say it was reassuring, his arms, his will. Then she stopped saying anything, but he feels she loves him, that often it even makes her weak at the knees. She tries to disengage herself, but he's insistent and forces a knee between her thighs.

"Shit, let go of me!"

"But you're my wife, aren't you? Fuck! I'm still entitled to fuck my wife!"

She tries to push him away with her slender arms but without result, so she wrinkles her nose with almost acted-out disgust, overdoing it. He's still hard and large, and won't let her go. As she struggles to break free, she rubs herself against his knee, despite herself. That excites him, so she slaps him. His breath is heavy with alcohol, his panting grows quicker. He lifts Séverine's skirt and pulls down her pants; she slaps him again. Manuel's large head barely stirs under her blows. Séverine stifles a cry by biting his bull neck violently. He takes the bite for an encouragement, an admission. She feels the grainy wall against her back. Manuel pushes into her so hard that she lets him come in, opening wider so as to avoid the pain, her thighs lifted, her shins resting on his back.

Sometimes, she imagines someone else, someone who doesn't exist and who would want her for the first time. He has no face or definite shape. Not an athlete or an actor but perhaps a blend of the two, with something new and inexpressible she yearns for without knowing it. A man who can dance, perhaps. Her purple pants, hanging from one of her ankles, are swaying in time with Manuel's buttocks, and this makes her want to cry. She manages to put one foot on the floor, like a thread reconnecting her to the world. Apart from that, her back is knocking against the wall, but it's not too painful – movements that set a rhythm and tilt her body under his desire. She can smell the discharge of familiar sweat, and the urgency of a helplessness she cannot give a name to makes her close her eyes. Séverine keeps replaying the words she fed Charlotte: she loves her life, she wouldn't change any of it for the world, and with Manuel things are as hot as in the beginning.

The Wretched of the Earth

As a child, Céline used to like crunching unripe, soft almonds. It was supposed to make her sick, but she never was. Green and downy, clusters of them would hang on the way to school. Céline would shell them with her teeth. Now the kernels no longer interest her, and their milky flesh seems bland. She just about enjoys cracking a few dried shells with a stone once the almonds are ripe. And not so much at that. The very gesture feels obsolete, a childhood gesture she discarded after she learned to put on make-up. Only Jo still gets excited when she finds twin fruits inside the shell and badgers her sister to play at Philippine, a stupid game where each swallows one of the pieces and, the next day, has to be the first one to yell "Good morning, Philippine", so her wish comes true. Kids' stuff. She remembers it because of the almond trees lining the long path between the main road and her grandparents' house.

In her grandmother's impeccably tidy kitchen, Céline has filled a flask of coffee for the workers, like she does every morning. She's slipped pieces of bacon and cheese, bread and a bottle of wine into the basket. The dog was attacking a bone, she could hear it through the open window, panting and growling at the end of its chain. To avoid the animal as she came out, she's dashed straight between the two hackberry bushes in the courtyard and gone to give their break to the wretched of the earth working in the apple tree field.

"Why do you insist on bringing us bacon when three quarters of us don't eat it?" Saïd asks, rummaging through the basket.

"It's not me, it's my grandmother."

"She does it on purpose."

"Yes, probably."

He takes a piece of cheese and eats it without bread. "I guess they'll never change."

"Bastards…" an old Algerian whispers as he opens the bottle of wine.

"But you do enjoy the bacon and the wine, you pig," Saïd exclaims, laughing.

"I'm Kabylian, I know what's good. But what they're trying to do, son, is to piss us off."

Céline doesn't like that. "Yeah, but they do give you work. Nice, considering they're bastards."

The Kabylian smiles at Céline, apparently weighing the words about to come out. The light digs into his wrinkles and he squints in the sunlight. Other workers approach and help themselves from the basket. They unroll their bodies, stretch and focus their eyes on the boss's granddaughter, sitting on a mound like a pot-bellied icon. She doesn't know what they think of her. The old man leans towards her. He gives off a slightly sour smell of sweat, full of tiredness. "Do you know what your grandfather did last year?"

"Why are you telling her this?" Saïd pleads.

"Why shouldn't I? She should know, she's not a kid any more. She might even think it's acceptable or clever."

"Stop it, Céline's not like that."

He adds something in Arabic which Céline doesn't understand.

"What did my grandfather do?"

Saïd shuts his mouth, his silence the signature of his surrender.

"He hired some illegals for the harvest," the old man resumes. "All the harvest. Of course, they were happy. He even let them sleep under the porch roof, with the tractor. They worked as though their lives depended on it, because their lives *did* depend on it."

"All right, Shems," Pascal, who has also approached, grumbles. "That's enough."

They all seem to know the story. But they're waiting to see how Céline will react.

The old Kabylian has a sip of wine straight from the bottle before carrying on. He gauges his effect, anger simmering behind his words and savouring the trick of the storyteller as the others gather around him.

"Those fuckers picked the grapes in record time. They were super-motivated. Your grandfather was the first one in the region to put them in the vats. And you know what he did after the harvest?"

Céline knows perfectly well he's not waiting for an answer. Still, she shakes her head, so he can carry on.

"He warned police headquarters and the gendarmerie."

Shems takes an unfiltered Gauloise from a crushed packet. The tip is bent, so he smooths it before putting it in his mouth. The smell of dark tobacco makes the girl nauseous as she waits to understand, although she's already understood but is milking it a little. "Some of them managed to run away across the fields and hide. The others were arrested. What's neat is that, all of a sudden, your grandfather doesn't need to pay them."

Céline is visibly affected. She can't work out if she's shocked or not, or if she should be. After all, she's heard about Arabs, Romas and Jews, and it's often them who stir the shit. Just look at all the terrorist attacks – she also watches TV.

It's all a bit confusing, but she honestly doesn't give a shit. A tooth for a tooth, and there's no smoke without fire, or something like that.

She doesn't say anything. She just feels her childhood packing its bags, along with fresh almonds and secrets spat out like phlegm.

Anything or Anybody

The kid has dry snot stuck to his cheek. Séverine crouches to wipe his face. In the village school where she works, Séverine doesn't just serve meals with a paper cap on her head. She also looks after the kids during playtime while the teachers are smoking their cigarettes in the parking area, and helps out during classes: she puts away the games, blows snotty noses, dabs scraped knees with red cotton wool and counts to make sure all the round-edged scissors are there. She hands the children to their parents after school. She doesn't mind. It's a job. Badly paid and exhausting, but so vital that she can't see how they could dispense with her. Naturally, she sometimes dreams of something else. But she doesn't know what.

She doesn't stop in the summer. The outdoor centre replaces school but it's the same kids, the same company that provides the meals, and playtime is longer.

She pushes the kid towards his mother, who quickly shoves a bun in his mouth. Séverine knows the boy's mother, of course, she's the younger sister of a high-school friend; except for American retirees and holidaying Parisians, she knows everybody here, and that's the problem.

"I heard about your daughter."

Séverine makes a U-turn, her face not very friendly, but the other woman isn't discouraged.

"If you need anything at all —"

"Like what?"

The mother's smile freezes and turns into an embarrassed laugh. "I don't know."

"If you don't know, why are you talking?"

The young woman pulls her kid towards her like a shield. She suddenly has a fleeting but clear picture of Séverine in year ten, while she was starting in year seven, a little girl lost amid all the ruthless savagery of preadolescence. Once, Séverine even made a female student supervisor cry. Self-confident and triumphant, she chose her friends and enemies from the jungle where she reigned. Back then, when she had reigned.

"I just wanted to help."

"We don't need anything or anybody."

When she gets home, she finds Jo in the kitchen. Feet on the table, her daughter is putting paprika crisps into the oven after dipping them in yoghurt.

"I've never understood how you can eat that."

Johanna turns away. "I put the dishwasher on."

Séverine starts emptying it, hanging the saucepans on the wall above the sink in order of size.

"Why are you so angry with Céline?"

The teenager's voice echoes in the silence of the kitchen, interrupted only by the sound of Pyrex plates her mother is now stacking up in the sideboard. Séverine purses her lips and her cheeks move as though she's chewing her words before spitting them out. "She deserves it."

Jo watches her, her and her staring eyes, suddenly lost in the cracks in the wall. "I don't understand."

"There's nothing to understand. Life's not like a fairy

tale for silly girls. Life hurts. You're younger, and yet I see you already know that. No point deluding yourself because then, in the end, it's worse."

She finishes putting the plates away, rubs her thumb over the embossed poppies and the hollow edges.

Jo rinses her bowl by hand in the sink, without answering. Her mother continues. "You shouldn't hang around so much with Saïd."

"Why? What have you lot got against Saïd?"

"Me, nothing. But your father is being stupid enough at the moment without you adding fuel to the fire."

"We've been friends for ever."

"You're not kids any more, and I don't know how he could afford to buy his car, but considering his wages as a farmworker —"

"So?"

"He's bound to be wheeler-dealing."

"As if you care about his wheeler-dealing. Papa does cash-in-hand work every other weekend, but if Saïd has some money, then he must be wheeler-dealing."

"That's not what I said."

"Actually, you did. That's exactly what you said."

Séverine sighs. She looks at her daughter and her furious eyes. Such an alien, such a strange gaze. After all, she couldn't care less if Jo hangs around with Saïd, or anybody else actually. She just wants to be left alone. She wishes she could have come home to an empty house, not had to talk or listen. She just wanted to be alone, that's all.

She feels immense relief when Jo goes up to her room. Pointing the remote at the screen like a weapon, Séverine lies down on the sofa. Dreading the arrival of the other two, she glances at the Mickey Mouse clock – another ugly thing she's never been able to get rid of. An hour of calm. She turns up the sound.

Corso Fleuri

The sound system blasts out a song by Louane that echoes through all the town loudspeakers. Jo wishes she could find the source of this crime and pull out the wires. She can't, and every time she hears the intro she pictures the singer being murdered, a bloodbath and torn vocal cords. The problem is that no village dance, no public event escapes her repertoire this summer; it's a curse that apparently won't be lifted until the autumn.

"Come on, you're exaggerating," Saïd says, laughing. "It's not that awful."

"I'd sooner have the old Tarantula dance tune."

Céline starts singing the lyrics she knows by heart into her sister's ear, enunciating every syllable, yelling the tune of the chorus.

"Stop it, you're pissing me off."

Still, it makes her laugh. It's good to see her sister messing about, her shoulders glowing with light, in the middle of the crowd. A saving grace. It makes her feel like everything can still be spared, summer and its consequences.

Rue Gambetta is echoing with the sounds Johanna despises, while dozens of groups cross paths, size one another up or merge on an afternoon that promises to be festive despite musical schisms and the bad blood between gangs who at present are casually eyeballing each other. Here, people still put on their Sunday best when they get the opportunity. Isle-sur-la-Sorgue, on the last day of July, and the *corso fleuri* is on, with boats parading along the river to the cries of the residents. Long barges manoeuvred with poles, unstable *Nego Chin* fishermen's boats buckling under the weight of flowers.

When Jo, Céline and Saïd were children, dozens of century-old plane trees had lined the river Sorgue in the very heart of the town. A nasty plant disease had forced the council to uproot every tree; the shores were then turned into esplanades. Nowadays, the walkers standing on the edge of the water to watch the boats go by quietly roast. Isle-sur-la-Sorgue is small, but not as shabby as Cavaillon. Perhaps it's the river, which crosses the town and displays its translucent shallows and its bed of soft algae, that gives it its old-fashioned charm. Or else the second-hand market and its tourists. Still a few squares with cobbles and high schools of a level not quite as low as those in Cavaillon. Two sister towns and yet there's no comparison. Even Jo knows that – the setting matters, nothing new in that. The kids yell, naked legs in the stream, whenever a new boat drifts by. There are themes, just like with floats, only on the water. One year, the girls took part. They were on an Egyptian boat, their eyes darkened, triangles at the corners of their eyelids like fake prepubescent Cleopatras. At first it was good fun but after a while it got boring, playing mini figureheads on that rather unsteady barge. The following summer, they chose to stay on dry land, alternating applause and mockery at the drifting floats displaying different countries' colours or a theme. One summer after another, they've chosen to chill out with their mates, with cans and giggles under the disapproving eyes of the riverside residents.

Besides, the three of them are now heading towards the barge that welcomes the gang every year. It's not deliberate, just a reflex. The village lot and a few hangers-on from the technical college, most of whom live in Cavaillon, will be there.

It's Lucas who sees them first. Sitting side-saddle on his moped, he reacts with surprise and joy when he sees Céline, but then pulls himself together and puts on a mask of indifference over his handsome face, which is studded with light-red patches. He massages the back of his neck, unsure of what to do: say hello or not, come up with a clever crack, an insult, pick a fight or vanish behind his mount. Ève and Vanessa, the ones Céline no longer speaks to, notice them. Manon gives a little shriek when she recognizes Céline. Unlike the other girls, Manon keeps sending her friend concerned messages every day. Then Enzo smiles at her, like before, so she turns to Saïd and her sister, her eyes shining, her hands nervous and all over the place – forehead, hair, ears, the bottom of her bag.

"I'm going to talk to Manon."

"Are you sure?" Johanna hisses.

She and Saïd watch her walk up to the others, belly forward, an unwelcome, bulky appendage. The time for resuming her position as queen is over, so now it's just a matter of existing.

"I don't understand why she even gives these shitheads a second thought."

"They're her mates, Jo."

"They're morons."

Jo doesn't approach. She looks at them, one by one, as they lift their cans to their lips, work their hips and arms and overdo their laughter. She sticks her hands into the back pockets of her shorts and does a U-turn.

*

On the other bank, Patrick is watching the girls. He's sitting on a café terrace, drinking a *perroquet* cocktail. It's Sunday, there's no work scheduled, so it's just an idle, hot day; it's good. He's spruced himself up, scrubbed flakes of paint and concrete from under his nails with a brush. He fiddles nervously with his swizzle stick, a naked woman on top of the orange plastic tube. Patrick absently rubs the pin-up's miniature hips with his thumbs. Valérie is saying something, telling some unpleasant story about the sorting manageress, a bitch who docked their pay because of a cigarette break that went on a bit too long. It was supposed to be temporary, the salad-sorting at Crudettes, because she was hoping to find something else but have a kid first, except that the kid never came and she ended up keeping her job. But with the latest round of restructuring, she doesn't know if she can stay at Crudettes. She's scared of being on the next redundancy list, so better not take long cigarette breaks.

Patrick's not listening. He pretends to, punctuating pauses with encouragements, smiling at no one in particular. He points his nervous profile right and left, his nose like a blade, smoothing his curls with the flat of his hand. The kid never came, and not for want of trying. Valérie counted the days, wrote dates in red pen on schedules where fucking had become reproduction-focused intercourse. The doctors searched, analysed and questioned. They couldn't work it out. As far as Valérie was concerned, everything was working to perfection, a well-oiled machine and a welcoming uterus. She'd been entitled to one treatment, just to increase their chances, but nothing. Not even a blighted ovum or an early pregnancy that ended in a miscarriage.

The doctors couldn't see what was going awry, Patrick's tests were also good despite a few weak sperm, a specialist had said, and he hadn't gauged the effect of these few words. He'd added that it was very common, that there was nothing to worry about, that it would in no way prevent them from conceiving a child. But his pride, for God's sake.

Anyway, they were still together, and that was as strange as it was logical – with a twisted logic, full of regrets disguised as fatigue, as familiar, reassuring resentment.

Valérie is sweating in her puff sleeve blouse, and there are dark haloes at her armpits. What with the treatment and the waiting, she has slid into this not altogether unpleasant, soft body, a valley of rounded flesh that's just a little too bulky to be attractive.

They gave up on the kid. At least that's what they say, putting on a fatalistic front. They've even taken to extolling the virtues of not having a child, and laying it on a bit thick whenever friends complain about theirs, going on about how lucky they are as though they'd actually made the decision.

Parisians sit at the tables nearby and express surprise at how cheap things are *in the provinces.* They're as happy as settlers.

Patrick looks at Manuel's daughters. Céline is sitting on the edge of the water, a hand on her belly. She tosses her hair back. It's lovely, but not like before. Patrick looks at every boy who's with her, squinting to see them better.

"Are you listening to me?"

"Sorry."

Valérie finally swivels round. When she turns back to face Patrick, she's no longer smiling. Her mouth is a little twisted and she questions her husband with her eyes, then asks, "You think Manuel knows they're here?"

He shrugs and finishes his drink. He fiddles with his phone and looks again at Saïd and Jo heading into the side road, towards the parking area by the dam. A huge *Nego Chin* full of dancers cuts off his view.

Inside the Audi that smells brand new with a whiff of weed, Saïd is trying to make up for his hesitations last time. He can see it won't be straightforward. It's always complicated with girls. And even more so with Jo. There's her constant irritability and that urge to go check out someplace else to see if the world is worth the bother. In his heart, he vaguely understands her urge, but he doesn't believe it's any better elsewhere. It's six of one, half a dozen of the other. You just have to give things time to smooth themselves out, and you can dig yourself a comfortable little hole, even in a shithole. Besides, what can she possibly know about life at fifteen? Actually, he's glad he's three years older; it sometimes gives him the feeling he's in charge. Girls his own age scare the shit out of him, and he hasn't sucked the blood from their scraped knees. When you fall off the bike on narrow, bumpy roads, you develop a bond.

But right now he's getting a bit pissed off. She's still sulking. "It's a nice car, though, isn't it?" he says, tentatively.

Jo darts him a look without passion. She's drinking her beer like a disenchanted rock chick, one leg folded under her, the other resting on the glove compartment. She throws her head back when she blows out the smoke from her cigarette. A bit too theatrical, but effective. Saïd laughs nervously.

"Go ahead, act like you don't care."

"I don't care."

"Oh really?"

She sighs like a woman worn out. "Yeah, I don't care about your car."

"Is there a problem?"

"No. Yes."

"Is it your sister?"

"I don't know."

Then, as if stung by a horsefly, she grows restless and looks for the button to open the automatic window. "Can't breathe in here."

"Wait, I've got air conditioning."

"Oh, great…"

Jo's sarcasm hurts Saïd. This car cost him an arm and a leg. He's proud of it. Jo fixes her odd eyes on the front window. Her mind is elsewhere and he's getting fed up.

"What are you thinking?" he asks.

"About Antigone."

She's being hard on him today.

"Shall we go somewhere else?"

"Do you know who Antigone is?" Jo asks.

"Shall we find a quiet spot?"

"You don't know who she is."

"What?"

"Antigone. You don't know who she is."

"Shit, I don't care! A mate of yours?"

He knows it's not the right answer, he knew it before he spoke, but she was really getting on his nerves. Whenever she puts on her I-know-more-than-you-do airs, whenever she rubs it in, he could just slap her. And then there's her bare skin, the hollow in her collarbone, her legs, and he's sure she wants it too, so why is she provoking him? Most of the time he feels comfortable with her. And then sometimes he feels like she takes over and he follows, not quite believing

118

it. It should really be the other way round, is what he sometimes tells himself, not quite understanding.

Jo kicks off her sandals, scrunches against the door, knees to her chin. She finally unclenches her jaw. "Where do you want to go?"

Her changing the subject makes him feel a little more relaxed. And he's happy to take her wherever she likes, there are loads of quiet spots he knows well, they'll find one of those.

As soon as he turns the key in the ignition, "Paper Planes" by M.I.A. bursts out of the speakers and makes them both jump. Saïd leans over to turn down the sound. They don't hear the first knock on the driver's side front door. It's only when the rear-view mirror explodes that they react.

"Are you fucking crazy!" Saïd yells, jumping out of the car.

Manuel stands facing Saïd, Patrick a little further away. "What are you doing with my daughter?"

"Fuck, Papa, this is insane!" Johanna roars, also getting out of the car. She stands facing her father.

Manuel grabs her by the wrist. "You're fifteen, so you keep your mouth shut. I'm still in charge."

Her father's grip on her wrist bone is like a wolf trap: except for chewing her own flesh, she can see no way of getting away from it. Except to bite his, perhaps – and she sinks her teeth into his hand. He lets go but lashes out with the back of his hand so hard she's in a daze, sitting on the gravel. She holds her chin and gingerly touches her nose with her fingertips, to check. There's no blood but it hurts, and she starts sobbing softly.

"Get back into your shitty car."

The father's voice is like a roar in her buzzing head, and Saïd looks at her, bites his lip powerlessly and clenches his fists.

"It's OK, Manuel, the little shit's leaving. You, fuck off," Patrick adds.

Saïd spits on the ground at Manuel's feet. "It's the second time you've done it, and now you've touched my car, so —"

"So what?"

"We'll talk about it later."

"Yeah, right."

"Did you tell your mate how you supplement your wages?"

"Shut the fuck up!"

Saïd gets back into his car, raging like a trapped animal. "Fucking morons," he blurts, starting the engine.

Jo gets up, rubbing her thighs. Her face is sticky with tears and sweat; she rubs her eyes with the bottom of her T-shirt.

His mouth in a sudden snarl, Patrick goes up to Manuel. "What did he mean by that?"

"Don't know."

"Do you take me for an idiot?"

"Not at all —"

"Are you doing business with that Arab?"

"Fuck it, leave me alone."

Patrick takes his head between his hands. "You're out of your mind, Manuel. Seriously, what are you up to? And with that piece of shit? Are you crazy? Were you going to tell me?"

"Stop it, you're not my wife."

"We've been mates for twenty years, man. Twenty years! And you wheeler-deal behind my back with a kid who fucks your daughters?"

The fist breaks loose and smashes into Patrick's cheekbone. There's a soft, almost yielding crack. Patrick slowly massages himself then belts like a bull, head first into Manuel's stomach, his fists pummelling his ribs. Manuel staggers and catches Patrick bodily to make him let go.

But he can't; the other man is sinewy and insistent like a mosquito. So the dance continues, their feet raising dust like hooves, their heads red and sweaty, their fists clenched, their arms like lead, muscles tense. Manuel is the stronger one but Patrick is quick and furious about having been betrayed. It increases his strength. Their panting from the effort and the heat are like groans of love, or death rattles.

"Stop it!"

Jo's voice is like a wave. They can barely hear it. She has to shout two or three times before they break up, mouths frothy, noses wet, their breathing hoarse and irregular.

"Nobody's *fucking* me," Jo hisses. "You're morons."

She shakes her head like a little mule, her eyes full of tears she's holding back with all her strength because being a crybaby isn't her style. Crying from pain because of a blow is one thing, but otherwise you've got to keep your self-respect.

"But you're still in cahoots with him," Patrick insists, not letting go of his resentment, ready to fight again.

"We'll talk about it later, just the two of us."

The kid clearly didn't hear; Patrick realizes that, and their old fools' complicity immediately resurfaces, as solid as their anger. "You don't know these kinds of guys, Jo. You don't know what they're capable of."

"These kinds of guys?"

"When they're not wheeler-dealing, they go off to Syria or else get themselves blown up at airports."

"You two've totally gone round the bend."

"Just watch the news."

"You know nothing about life, you're fifteen years old."

"We know them, we work with them."

The two men shoot a volley of responses in front of an astounded Jo.

"For fuck's sake, we've been friends since kindergarten!" she says.

"Yes, but you're not at kindergarten any more."

The two old men present a united front, twenty years of friendship and bruises on their faces. *Twenty years of fucking stupidity,* Jo thinks. The arch of Patrick's eyebrow is bleeding a little. Like kids outside high school. Kids with the strength of men, playing at being men.

"You're in a muddle, you don't understand anything."

"You think you're more clever? I'm your father and I decide. I'm taking you back home."

Patrick tries to soften the order. "Come on, Jo, don't sulk, get into the pick-up, your father's right."

She gives him a look black with rage. She thinks about Saïd, who ran away and left her alone with these two fucking morons. She climbs into the pick-up and feels her phone vibrate. It's a text from Garance to arrange the date for the party. Next Saturday. In six days' time, she's going to a party with Garance and her friends. A cheerful uneasiness, a euphoria she hides as best she can, soothes her rage at being made to do something by her father right now.

Manuel gets in next to her. "Where's your sister?"

"No idea."

Arms crossed, Patrick stands next to the door. The blood has turned black at the corner of his eyebrow.

The two men still challenge each other with their eyes, then Manuel sighs. "I'll explain, Patrick. I'll explain tomorrow. We're not going to let a kid stir up shit between us."

Patrick's features relax at this renewed promise. Thick as thieves. For life, etc. He slaps the door with the palm of his hand the way you pat an animal. When the pick-up starts, he massages the back of his neck and his jaw, worried – practically certain – that his friend partly pulled his punches. That makes him feel uncomfortable. He'd rather his friend had punched him for real.

Friends for Life

If someone had asked Manuel when exactly they'd really become friends, he and Patrick, he'd have thought a long time, listed their countless joint memories, and, yes, perhaps he would have zoned in on that greasy, June '92 afternoon when, having skipped classes to go and watch *It* in Patrick's father's bedroom, he had finally managed to go all the way with Nathalie in the next room – Patrick had been championing his friend to his cousin for weeks, using his own charm and showering his pal with an aura of mystery and charisma. Or perhaps he would have chosen one of the many times when Patrick had covered for him with Séverine, when he'd lost his day's wages on lottery tickets at the bookie's. Or that time, much earlier on, when, hammered, they had both ended up in the principal's office, avoiding expulsion by a whisker, accomplices in drunkenness and defiance.

But if anyone had asked Patrick the same question, he would have said, without hesitation, that their friendship had become rock solid that day in November '90 when he'd introduced him to his mother.

The student supervisor had walked in in the middle of the class and whispered a few words to the history teacher, who'd immediately looked at Patrick. "Bardin, you're expected in the office."

Her tone had lost its usual severity, ritualized by the daily confrontation with the savage horde that made up this class of adolescents whose testosterone was in constant competition with their foolishness. At that moment, she'd softened the way you lower your guard, the school stage fading, overtaken by life. After a slight hesitation, she'd said, "Gomez, go with him."

Manuel had bounced up and grabbed his bag in the hope of not returning to class. It had been a good insight: neither of them had set foot in school again that day. Patrick's mother had tried to commit suicide again, using the TV cables to hang herself, and this time had nearly succeeded. It was a cousin who'd been able to intervene in time, when she had brought back home Patrick's little sister after an hour in the park. She'd come back early because of the rain. She'd shown remarkable nerve for a girl so young, by dialling the emergency number and that of the aunt, her fingers trembling and the little kid on her hip. She'd remember it for a long time, even after she settled into a new life, far from Cavaillon. Perhaps this event had played some part in her desire to escape. The body was lying at a funny angle, nothing to do with a rope tied to a beam and the chair kicked from under your feet like in films; Patrick's mother had twisted the cables around her neck without even unplugging them and thrown herself forward, on her knees, the weight of her upper body squeezing her trachea hard enough with the plastic casings to asphyxiate her. She'd taken a fair amount of sleeping tablets beforehand, to make it easier. She'd vomited a little. Then the firefighters had broken into the living room and fussed over her. They were still there when the two kids showed up. The aunt had called the school immediately, because at times like that, bringing the tribe, however unstable, together, was a reflex. Besides, as far as the aunt was concerned, the father was a waste of space. And Patrick agreed: his father was a waste of space, especially since he'd walked out on them.

There were no silver helmets or even a siren on the roof of their engine: the firefighters were used to it; it wasn't the first time, and – with any luck – it wouldn't be the last. They'd taken Patrick's mother away before the two teenagers' eyes. To the emergency room first, then definitely a period in psychiatric care. Patrick was used to it by now, and could manage without her as long as his aunt or his cousin took care of his sister. He could cope with the stale smell of dirt and the absence that verged on emptiness. That day, Manuel had stood staring at the recently dried vomit on the face of the woman others called *mad*. And at the rather disgusting apartment where he'd never yet been invited.

For a long time, Patrick wondered why he'd dragged his mate along that day, except for the opportunity of a day off school. Maybe it was time, maybe he needed someone to witness all that.

As far as he was concerned, it was at that moment that they had become as bound together as bricks glued with concrete. Because Manuel had kept his trap shut. Closed his eyes to the greasy, ugly apartment, and to his drowsy, crazy mother. Because after the firefighters had left, accompanied by the aunt, Manuel had picked up a video case from between two cushions on the sofa and suggested, like on any regular Wednesday, "Shall we watch *Terminator*?"

The Banks of the Durance

The cold, sticky fluid spread over Céline's belly has taken her by surprise. With expert gestures, the sonographer has smoothed the gel, pressing at times, insisting on certain areas. A little brusque, a little stiff, unnerved by the young age of her patient and the heavy, silent presence of her grandmother. Séverine has refused to come with her daughter. Work, she said, but Céline understood perfectly well.

They wanted to know and yet neither the old woman nor the young one said anything when the sonographer announced flatly, "It's a girl."

Curses come around again and again, it's the same principle, no way anyone could alter the course of things. In Céline's head, this life in her belly was only just becoming a reality, so the child's sex... But her grandmother gritted her teeth.

When they came out of the doctor's, the old woman went shopping. Céline went to join her sister in a special spot near the Durance, a soft river that runs beside the general lycée where Jo is going in September and Céline will never go. It's cool there. They say junkies come and shoot up here. You sometimes see prostitutes, the ones who can't afford to perform in a second-hand Clio on the edge of vineyard paths. You sometimes step on used condoms between the reeds and the gravelly riverbed. Nothing bucolic about it.

"So?"

"So what?"

"Is he in one piece? Not a crooked face like you?"

"She."

"Oh."

"Yeah. And fuck you."

There's not even enough energy for a row.

They don't look at each other, and instead direct their gazes to the polluted, glistening eddies, as if the other bank is more interesting, even though it's Orgon on the other side, a commuter town – a worse version of Cavaillon. No hope there; you must take the main highway that starts a hundred yards away and drive at least as far as Marseilles before you can even hope for an elsewhere that counts. They can hear the cars, the buzz of the roundabout that drowns out the river. At the heart of the roundabout there's a giant melon, replaced with a flashing Santa Claus from 2 December. From the cove where they're having a cigarette, throwing pebbles into the water, they can't see the road, or the Decathlon, or the McDonald's. They're just guessing.

"Would you have preferred a boy?"

Céline shrugs without answering.

"You don't care?"

"Don't know. Maybe. I don't know."

"What are you going to do?"

"What do you mean?"

"Will you go back to the lycée, afterwards?"

Céline shakes her hair and throws her cigarette into the Durance. "Makes me nauseous."

"The cigarette or the lycée?"

"You're a bitch. It's you who makes me nauseous."

They allow silence, familiar, to fall. There's a light breeze whistling through the reeds. Then Céline says, "I don't care about the lycée. I wouldn't have passed the professional Baccalauréat anyway. I don't care about quitting, in fact it's better for me. You're the family intellectual."

"What?"

"Look, you even hang out with the posh kids from Saint-Jo now."

"Shut the fuck up." Jo's laughter echoes softly; she leans back and lies down, resting on her elbows. "And you're going to work with our grandparents all your life, great."

"Maybe. In any case, Gran will be able to help me, because I'm not relying on Maman."

"Clearly not."

"I'll look for a job. If I get a place in the crèche, I'll work it out."

She says it calmly, just like that, but in truth she's almost relieved she doesn't have to go back to school. The day of the *corso fleuri*, she saw perfectly well that things had changed, and not for the better. Even Manon doesn't have a clue, gushing over Céline's belly, going crazy over the kid on the way, like *it's going to be great, babies are so cute, and you're so lucky!* Céline hasn't said anything, it was still better than the pity in other people's eyes, the embarrassed smiles that said she'd toppled into another world and there was no returning from there.

"And you're not going to give me a clue about the father?"

"No."

"Frankly, you could at least make him cough up." Jo's eyes search her sister, she insists with her gaze.

"Drop it. I don't want anything from him."

"Well, at least you seem to know who he is, which is comforting."

"Oh, fuck you, I'm not a tart."

Articulated lorries whizz across the bridge over the Durance; the girls follow the convoy with their eyes.

"Have you been to see Grandpa in hospital?"

"No, but I'll go soon."

"Shall we have a McDonald's?"

"Yeah, and then let's go back and doll up for your posh party."

Their gazes wander beyond the main highway. Seen from the cars, they're as tiny as mice.

Preparations

There are guys in the Docteur-Ayme housing complex who are ready to smash anyone's face in, given a chance. Saïd knows several like that. He was happy to make an effort because of Jo and Céline, but it's got out of hand now and the old guys are in for it. He can't stand up to them on his own, but next time he won't be alone. Of course, that'll put an end to his dealings with Manuel. But he knows people: on the business front, it won't be hard to find another builder ready to pinch two or three antiques from posh people's building sites. Sometimes, it's even more than posh – what do you call it when it's even more? Some of his mates would say *lucky bastards, dripping with money*. Saïd doesn't actually mind these people. They're a godsend for the survival of his job. As long as there are rich people, he'll be able to take advantage of them, get into the cracks and make everyone happy – while helping himself on the way. When all's said and done, just like Manuel and Patrick, Saïd is a small-timer: his profits would make the owners of even the smallest villa laugh themselves stupid. But he doesn't mind the order of things, and his greed is reasonable. A prudent young man adapted to his times. But on the other hand, he often has a sense of entitlement and feels the need to defend his territory. You don't touch his car, that's it. You don't threaten him like that. Saïd has respect for the old guys, especially for the father of his friends, but it's time to set boundaries and not let himself be trampled on, not let these guys treat him without respect. So he's called two of his mates and is waiting for them with determination. Three should be enough. Enough to make an impression on the other two, but not so many that it looks like a beating. He's waiting outside his house, leaning against his car while rolling a joint. Every now and then he glances at the damaged mirror that's hanging by its wires and feels anger bubble up. That's good. Small waves that keep up the impetus and reassure him his plan is justified. Of course, there's also the job at the farm, his seasonal work, and especially his mother's. But this is a matter between men, and Manuel wouldn't go and whine about him to his father-in-law. Or would he?

Another glance at the back of the car – he's doing the right thing, he's right. A long drag, his eyes shut. His friends won't be here for a while, so he's got time. The cat walks past, mewing, crazy-eyed: the stupid thing still hasn't worked out she'll never see her little ones again and has been looking for them everywhere for days. He grits his teeth – fuck, he doesn't care, after all it's an animal. Saïd blows out the thick smoke through his mouth and nose, thinking about Johanna's legs.

She couldn't make up her mind at first, and finally opted for a black T-shirt, denim shorts and Roman sandals. Then she put on make-up only to remove it all with cotton wool and cream and start again. The very fact of spending so much time on this and being unable to make up her mind has made her angry. Consequently, instead of enjoying herself, Jo is harbouring persistent irritability at the start of this evening, which she takes out on her sister. She finds it impossible simply to admit she's scared, scared of going to a party where she only has one friend, if that, scared she won't like the people, scared of not being liked. She thought she didn't care about all that.

"Are you really going to wear those things? Are you serious?" Jo looks at Céline and her red feather earrings.

"You don't like them?"

"They're ugly. They look like – don't know, don't like them."

"You're pissing me off. Always criticizing."

"No I'm not."

"Yes you are, and even more so since you made new friends."

"They're not my friends. And I didn't have to wait for them before I criticized your clothes."

"That's true, you're a real bitch."

"Or your slutty jewellery."

"At least a slut can put on her make-up."

A blend of defeat and childish laughter appears on Jo's face. She's really pretty when she smiles, with dimples like fish hooks in the hollows of her cheeks. As she gets older she'll probably be even more attractive than her sister, but you can't see it yet because she struggles to fully live in her own body.

"All right, help me, but don't put tons on."

In the corridor, there's the sound of their mother's footsteps when they thought they were alone. The door suddenly opens.

"You could knock."

"You expect me to ask permission, do you?"

"Well, yeah."

"Don't push it, Céline, and don't take that tone."

The kid holds her gaze, a final show-off of pride before yielding.

"Where are you going exactly?"

"To a party, in Gordes."

"Your new mates?" Séverine asks, jutting her chin at Johanna, who grunts to say yes.

The mother looks at Céline. "You're not going."

"What?"

"You're just not going."

Séverine realizes it's really stupid to argue that Céline should stay. With any luck, Manuel will hang out with Patrick after work; she often gives him grief because of it but, in truth, she quite likes it – to be alone and then give him grief. She wonders if she still has the power to stop her daughter from doing anything whatsoever without the support of paternal threat. She knows the answer.

Tears of rage appear in the corners of the teenager's eyes. "I'm sixteen!"

"You're sixteen and you're staying right here. Have you seen what you look like, with that belly?"

"So? Is it stopping me from partying and seeing people?"

"You're staying here, that's it."

Deep down, both mother and daughter know that Céline will go out anyway, through the window if she needs to. But at least they're pretending – it's important. Séverine turns to Jo, who's sitting on the bed, knees bent up, elbows resting on them. "Who are you going with?"

Jo wants to say they're going to the party in Saïd's car just to piss her mother off but she actually hasn't spoken to Saïd since the last time. She can't totally forgive him for having run away and left her alone with her father and Patrick. But, above all, even though she has trouble admitting it, she doesn't want to mess things up. As it is she's a bit worried about turning up there with her sister, but Saïd on top of that... She keeps telling herself that in any case he'd be bored, so no point in risking it. "Garance's sister is coming to pick me up in the car."

"Here?"

"No, in the village," Jo almost cries out, and there's anxiety in her reply.

Séverine is hurt by this, and remembers that at the same age she, too, preferred to wait for her friends at the bottom of the path rather than in the farm kitchen, under the old people's eyes. She wonders if she, too, is old now, and tightens her ponytail by parting it into two strands and pulling on them. "Stay the night there, if everybody's drinking."

Before she leaves the room, in a surge of emotion she can't explain, Séverine strokes one of the scarlet feathers dangling at her eldest daughter's ears. "They're pretty. They suit you."

When Jo comes out of the house, Saïd doesn't see her. He's got his back to her, thirty yards away, his buttocks pressed against the side of his car. Jo gives her sister a sign and walks quietly to the paved path. While waiting for Céline to climb out through the window, she watches a wave of bats skimming the tops of the cherry trees and diving under the roofs of the crumbling houses along the fields. It's like the flight of ashes over blazing paper. Jo quite likes that, it makes her a little sad, she doesn't know why, though it's not an unpleasant sensation. An interlude of pain and fulfilment – beauty often has that effect on her. She's still young: it will take some time before she's able to identify the inexpressible, these oases of the sublime amid the chaos, these fleeting instants that save you.

"What are you looking at?"

Céline wipes the sweat from her temples and above her lip, looking at her sister. A little out of breath, she starts talking, lifting her hair with one hand and securing it with a clip. "I almost can't get over the wall any more, with my belly."

"You've changed your earrings?"

"Maman thought they looked pretty. Made me suspicious."

In front of the cross at the entrance to the village, a white Laguna is waiting for them. Garance's sister is punctual.

The Foreman

It's been brewing since the morning: a crappy atmosphere and people talking behind his back, he's sure of it. Manuel looks at the others without warmth and works in silence. Every so often, Patrick taps him on the shoulder, but not too often, because there's still tension between them. Now he knows about the trafficking with Saïd, it's a bit better: Manuel explained on the way to the building site. He picked him up in his truck at the junction with Coustellet, outside the tobacconist, and came out with it on the way. *No Arab is going to mess up our friendship.* The other man didn't say anything, kept his teeth gritted and squinted at the end of the road while Manuel talked. And now, in between spadefuls of cement, Patrick can't help coming back on the offensive.

"Why didn't you tell me?"

"I don't know, the first time it was just on an impulse, and since the kid was working with second-hand goods, I mentioned it to him."

"You could have included me in the plan, you know I'm not exactly rolling in it."

"He said I should keep it to myself."

"Fuck, Manuel…"

"Yeah, I know, I know."

They fall silent; the afternoon sun is scorching their skin. Their backs are brown, like those of the Arabs.

"What are you going to do?"

"What do you mean?"

"With that little shit – what are you going to do?"

"I don't know. If it's him who did this to my daughter…"

He looks up to check if anyone else is listening.

The other builders aren't looking at him and their intention to avoid him – so as not to make him feel uncomfortable – is having the opposite effect. It's obvious everybody's been talking about the girl. Beautiful, on display before their eyes in her strappy tops and skinny jeans. Too pretty, no doubt. Manuel imagines them laughing at him behind his back. He's wrong. In fact, the men feel sorry for him and, among themselves, indulge in a few salacious remarks which they think are male-style compliments. Of course, Manuel wouldn't appreciate them, even though he sometimes makes the same cracks about the waitress at the Fin de Siècle, who's the same age as Céline. He doesn't make the connection.

"If he's the one who got Céline pregnant…" He keeps telling himself that, so the notion sinks in. "Fuck, if it's him… I'll kill him. I'll do a pretty job on that rat face of his."

When the owner pops out on the verandah right in the middle of the building site to see how the work's progressing, a frown runs a line across her pretty forehead. She's furious: the Italian tiles still haven't been laid around the edge.

What the fuck are these builders doing in her garden? Is she paying them to chat?

Manuel feels a surge of anger twisting his belly. He wishes he could rearrange her face, but he can't. Maybe because she's a woman. She's wearing a navy-blue swimsuit, a linen shirt that comes halfway down her thighs and a straw hat with a wide brim that hangs around her face, sullen with annoyance.

"Are you the foreman?"

"Yeah," Manuel mutters.

"Is it you who gives the orders to all the – the others?"

"That's me, yeah."

All of a sudden he's not feeling so cocky. And yet he's pleased that the boss has put him in charge of the site. But under the unfriendly gaze of the woman on her high horse, it's a pain to be forced to take responsibility. He'd happily tell it straight to this posh bitch. These marble slabs, a thousand euros a piece, are already sticking in his throat.

She pulls a face as she sees her heeled espadrilles sink into the loose soil.

"I'm warning you, if the terrace and the decorative pond aren't done in the next three days, I'm not sure I can pay you."

"Excuse me?"

"Look, my garden's been taken over for a month, the soil is dug up, I can't get to my terrace, not to mention the pool. It's 10 August!"

"Your daughter's getting married on the eighteenth, right?"

"It's not just about my daughter's wedding. It's about my holidays!"

Manuel looks at the rest of the team, the eight guys who keep working in silence, carefully listening to the exchange but looking like they don't give a shit.

"I'm going to Menton shortly, for two days. By the time I'm back, the work will be completed."

"I'm not sure —"

"Your boss said it would be finished by the beginning of August."

Clearly wanting to get a clear, humble response, and since Manuel's teeth are still gritted, the woman takes her phone out of her shirt pocket. "Shall I call him to remind him, or do you think you can speed things up yourself?"

"It's fine." An abrupt bark.

He waits for her to go back into the coolness, behind the curtains, before he calls the men.

"Let's get on with it, guys. You heard her."

"And who's going to pay the overtime? Her?"

"Fuck, Gypsy, shut it!" Manuel cuts in. "You've been with us two weeks and I haven't seen you stay past six o'clock once, so don't push it."

The young guy swears and spits. His wife's just had the second one, so it'd be nice if he went home in the evening.

"Oh really? Your second one and your wife? And is it your wife you were going to see at the bookie's yesterday? Is she working behind the bar now?"

The guy approaches, clearly not amused. The others put down their tools. Manuel isn't really cut out to be a boss. Those who know him have no objections, he's strong and capable, and besides it's temporary, but the young Gypsy hasn't been here long. For him, Manuel is just a boss, and he doesn't like bosses.

Before the Gypsy has time to stand in front of Manuel to challenge him to a fight, two guys grab him around the waist to prevent him from doing something stupid. "Leave him," Manuel hisses. "This way we can also talk about the copper pipes that went missing two days ago —"

"Stop it, Manuel," Patrick says. "The blonde's watching. She'll call the boss if things get out of hand."

Holding the phone, she's clutching the curtain, eyes open wide, waiting for just one sign of violence to call the police – even before she contacts the boss. Manuel spreads his hands, lifts his palms high and gives the owner a glance. "Don't worry, he has a bit of a temper. It's OK, don't worry. It's all fine, see?"

She disappears behind the curtain. The men are uneasy. Motionless in the clammy heat, they're waiting like children, exchanging worried and insolent glances. They slowly get back to work. The Gypsy tries to challenge Manuel with his eyes before buckling down but it's too late, the moment's gone, Manuel's already forgotten about him.

They work for an hour or two, until the surrounding hills lose some of their glare and start to turn golden. The owner reappears, dressed this time, with sunglasses on her head and holding a handbag. She doesn't smile or say hello to anyone. She just walks up to Manuel and hands him the house keys, a bundle held together by a horseshoe that weighs heavily in his palm.

"Two days. I'm trusting you."

Her exasperated tone suggests the contrary, but she doesn't really have a choice. Nobody would take over halfway through the job if she sacks this team. Besides, the new ones wouldn't be any better, she knows that, God, they're so slow; after all, it's not rocket science to finish a job in a timely manner. These southerners, it's as though everything goes over their heads: priorities, delays, respect. She gets into the grey Audi, tired. She rummages through her bag and finds her codeine tablets, swallows one dry while waiting for the automatic gates to let her out.

The men all straighten up to see the car vanish at the top of the path, between the vineyards.

*

The gear has been cleared away in silence. The cement mixer and the rest: locked up in the garage. Around here, anything that can be stolen is, they all know it, and no builder would be careless enough to leave his tools lying around on a site. Everyone's gone home, nobody mentioned anything, and this long evening silence has weighed heavily. What they should have done, as they often do in such cases, was to go down into town and all drink together until they were wasted – but nobody suggested it. It's not the first time an owner has got them with their backs against the wall, that's not the problem. The problem is Manuel and that swelling powerlessness that makes them all dubious. If one of them – and not the frailest one – cracks, it means none of them can be spared. So they put a distance between them, like a protective border. Except Patrick, who despite the silence managed to drag his friend to Robion, a commuter village but with a nice bistro. They've downed a few *mauresque* cocktails at the Petit Cheval bar without saying a word. And yet the tension won't relent. Manuel's foot is fidgeting nervously against the rail on the floor. He turns his glass abruptly, compulsively, the way you wind up a watch. When he stretches his hand to pay, the landlord approaches and refuses, *it's on me*, he says, but six glasses is quite a lot and Manuel doesn't like it.

"Is this fucker feeling sorry for me or what?"

"Stop it, he likes you, that's all."

But Manuel sees eyes and laughter everywhere, and an insult in every kindness. Every man he comes across who knows about it gives him the impression of having fucked his daughter. "I've got some whisky in the car," he finally says. "Let's go to my place."

They say goodbye to the other drinkers by tapping on their own foreheads, tipping imaginary hats they've never worn.

They drive in silence, fast. They pass a white Laguna but nobody, in either car, realizes who is who. In any case, it doesn't matter, it's just an inconsequential coincidence.

When they reach the estate, it's almost dark and their headlights take in Saïd, leaning against his car. Alone.

The Long Night

"Brilliant, you were able to come! And you're here with…"

"My sister, Céline."

In a wet white two-piece swimsuit, clutching the villa gate, Garance can't help staring, eyes wide, at Céline's full body, a T-shirt with *Love don't pay the bills* stretched over her belly. She wavers, searches Céline's body language for a sign to guide her reaction, whether she should be excited or not, and to help her find the right words. As she can't think of anything to say, Garance makes up for it with a smile full of kindness, the way people can when life has often been kind to them. She shakes her drenched hair and smooths it with her palms.

"Come in. We've put the buffet outside. For now everyone's bathing. Did you bring your swimsuits?"

The girls follow and discover a hundred-foot mosaicked pool filled with young people in swimwear, jumping into the turquoise water. Night is falling.

"I'm going to turn on the floodlights," Garance says.

The girls follow her with their eyes as, blonde and perfect, she runs into the house.

"Do you know the others?"

Jo tackles the mass with her eyes, sweeps over it without really looking. "The guy smoking in the deckchair over there. And the two girls laughing, with their legs in the water. I've met them once."

"He's not bad-looking. What's his name?"

"Côme."

"Huh?"

"Côme."

They fall silent. Céline goes to the buffet to fetch two beers. Glances travel to her, to her belly, her eyes, her belly, her breasts, then back to her belly. The conversations are half-hearted. She says hello then takes the tops off the beers with a cigarette lighter, aware of being watched. The crimped tops bounce on the ground and roll towards the pool. She doesn't bend down to pick them up.

Jo's feeling hot and her heart is beating fast. She suddenly wants to run away but the large swimming pool is beckoning her to plunge into the blueness, thwart the sweat and the prickling at the roots of her hair. Her sister hands her a beer.

The beams flood out from the bottom of the pool, splashing faces with a cinematic turquoise. A collective cry greets the light, and a handful of bathers leap into the water. They're good-looking, all of them, and healthy, and that seems banal. Toned, smooth, tanned bodies meet and stick together in a joyous dance of bubbling hormones. Côme comes up to them and holds out his glass to clink with their beers. On his feet, he's very tall, a head taller than Jo, and has a badminton player's muscles. Céline smiles at him.

"I'm going to change in the bathroom," Jo murmurs.

Côme giggles with his head cocked to the side, dimples in his face, still childlike despite his body language.

"Don't go into the downstairs one, it's engaged... Go up to the first floor, at the end of the corridor, third door on the left." He says that to Jo as she's walking away, not taking his eyes off Céline.

In the house, Jo acts as though she's seen it all before. Tense and wary, she looks at the corner sofas in this thousand-square-foot lounge, the double bass leaning against the wall, and its scores, messy on top of a chest of drawers. She's forgotten Côme's advice, and remembers only once she's outside the bathroom door, alerted by the panting. The girl is squealing softly and the door is ajar. From what Jo can tell, it sounds pleasant. She glances inside: a tanned, smooth back and a girl's legs welded to the guy's hips. She meets the gaze of the girl, who doesn't seem embarrassed. On the contrary; her pupils are dilated, and she suddenly laughs. *She's stoned*, Jo thinks, oddly relieved that it's not Garance. She feels pity for this girl, stupid enough to get fucked in full view and against a sink, seen by other people. As if she didn't know that a reputation sticks so firmly that it can make you into what other people want. Jo feels pity, but even so her inner thighs warm up strangely, and she stays there, rooted, a little longer than she should, fascinated by the couple's mechanics.

When she finally leaves, the images follow her, like the girl's laughter. And, like an echo, she hears the guy's voice: "What's the matter?"

"It's nothing, carry on, don't stop."

Jo speeds up, wanders past the kitchen, where other young people are bustling about, heaping food onto plates and laughing so loudly that she also feels like laughing, though she doesn't know why. But she's not friends with them, so she walks down a corridor lined with bookcases, crushed by titles she doesn't know. Going upstairs, she pretends she's a princess and imagines she's in her own home. But that doesn't actually work – she shakes her head and instead thinks about a raging fire.

She half opens doors to a series of bedrooms with ecru bedspreads and finally finds the second bathroom, as large as a living room, with a bath and twin basins.

In the free-standing mirror, she looks at herself critically and slowly undresses. The house is so large that the sounds don't even travel this far.

In the muffled silence, in her panties, she rummages through the bathroom drawers. Creams, perfumes, tablets. Soft white towels, folded like in a shop. She stops her raiding.

Her buttocks against the sink, she slides her hand to her sex without removing her pants: a pretence – the fabric barrier against her hand gives her a sense of innocence, of being secretive with herself. Lips swollen and moistened by the to-ing and fro-ing of her fingers, she thinks about the couple downstairs. And a little bit about Saïd. Jo arches her back and clenches her legs at the same time, and breathes deeply but without moaning – she knows the art of concealment. Sharing a room with her sister for fifteen years, she's had to learn to be discreet. Fifteen years of not having a place to herself, of hearing everything through walls as thin as cardboard, fifteen years of dreaming about intimacy. Now she knows how to do it, anywhere, anytime. She's even on occasion made herself come in public when she's really bored in class, by gritting her teeth and clamping her thighs together. But sometimes, when there's the chance of an empty space, a room just for herself for a few minutes, she takes advantage.

"Get in."

Saïd looks at the two men, unconcerned. His friends are on their way, he's feeling strong. He doesn't answer and shakes his head, laughing.

"Get in, I said." Hoarse, raspy with hostility, Manuel's voice bursts out in the darkness. Holding the handle of his pick-up truck door, it's as though he thinks Saïd will obey if he raises his voice like with a spoiled kid. He nods at the inside of the truck, teeth gritted. "Do we have to come and fetch you?"

"I'm not moving from here and I swear —"

Manuel lets go of the door. Before Saïd can see anything coming, Manuel's foot crushes his balls violently. Blinding pain: he bends in half, breathless. The pain is such that he staggers and falls to his knees, hands cupped over his genitals, eyes welling with tears. In his head are a thousand insults, unable to come out because he's drooling and on the verge of fainting. Patrick lifts him by one arm, Manuel by the other. They pull him to the pick-up, feet and knees dragging in the dust. Hands still securely at his groin, Saïd opens his eyes wide despite the tears. It's all very quick. The two men heave him into the front; Patrick walks around and sits on his right, while Manuel starts the engine.

"Motherfuckers!" Saïd finally hisses, curled up between the two builders.

"Shut the fuck up."

Manuel drives fast, eyes on the road, the yellow lights sweeping the asphalt.

Saïd realizes between spasms of pain that his mates are going to arrive too late. What he still can't understand, on the other hand, is why these two guys hate him, and what they really want from him. It's true he's made some money, but for sure nothing to buy a villa with. Side gigs, little somethings that are better than nothings, but not heaps of money either. There's his car, of course. He wasn't trying to show off, it's just that he's always liked cars and it's the first time he's been able to afford one that wasn't shit. And yet his contacts have always told him: don't act clever, keep your head down, and it'll be all right. Mustn't change your habits, especially in a village. People don't like it when you get out of your box, it reminds them they're in one.

They drive for quite a while, in silence. Saïd is in pain. He catches his breath but it's still hurting. He touches, strokes, weighs: everything is still where it should be, and it's an odd kind of relief.

The road becomes rougher, the wheels bite into slopes of dry grass that would catch fire at the first cigarette butt. Manuel seems to know where he's going. He finally pulls up to a large, imposing, outrageously elaborate gate. He takes out of his pocket the jangling bunch of keys with the horseshoe at the end – his hands are shaking slightly – and activates the gate to open.

It's about 11 p.m. when, after driving slowly down the carpet of gravel, the pick-up truck parks by the garage door.

Céline is laughing at everything Côme says. He's full of humour, but she doesn't get all his jokes. He knows this and is doing it deliberately. He likes it when this girl cracks up every time he comes up with something. He suddenly feels alone but enjoys being outside the situation and making himself laugh. He enjoys his superior solitude, it's his fix. Besides, this pregnant girl who's popped out of nowhere is very attractive. Not one of his own kind, of course, and he, a boy from a good family, is oddly excited by that. And since his intelligence affords him the luxury of somewhat despairing cynicism, he allows himself to think that, yes, it would be fun to fuck her, with that big belly and that coarseness that surfaces whenever she laughs. It would be great, decadent, new. He's so bored.

"What is it? Why are you looking at me like that?"

Céline chuckles and starts on the third beer Côme hands her.

He feels disgusting, and he finds that delicious.

Some friends of his have come up to them, interested in the new girl. Côme lets them, because he also likes having an audience. It's a piece of cake: he feels strong, ready to play executioner and protector. At the same time, he's never forced anyone, right? He's sure she wants it, that she'll ask him. The prospect is driving him insane, and he's getting a bit hard in his midnight-blue Speedos.

Drinking her beer in small sips, Céline thinks she was right to come. It's a nice change from seasonal workers, and these people can certainly party. She sees neither contempt nor judgement in their eyes; she thinks they're gorgeous and funny and they seem to find her attractive.

Céline is sixteen.

The Voltaire armchair is perfect. Manuel's taken it from the lounge and carried it to the garage while Patrick was holding Saïd down on the ground, one arm twisted behind his back. The boy didn't immediately realize how serious the situation was and kept arguing, humiliated but not worried yet. At least not very.

Manuel unrolls a length of insulating tape, binds Saïd's wrists tighter to the armrests, then bandages him around the waist with the rest.

"Don't, Manuel. Fuck, you're insane, I don't know why you..."

Patrick takes a gulp of whisky, puts the bottle in a corner, and picks up a PVC pipe with one hand. He has a strange expression as he looks at the young man tied to the Voltaire armchair. It's almost funny, his head pressed against the red velvet with a halo of upholstery tacks, his arms on the carved wooden armrests.

"Did he say anything?"

Manuel shakes his head. His mouth is twitching with a nervous tic, a mechanical smile that lifts only one corner. An uncontrollable movement he feels throbbing in his cheek. Distraught, Saïd looks at one, then the other. "Shit, you're mental, I haven't done anything! You hear me?"

"What? What did you say?"

Manuel drinks from the bottle then puts it down on the ground.

"Did you just call us mental?"

The PVC pipe comes down to crack the boy's cheekbone.

"Bastards, fucking shits, you don't know what's waiting for you —"

"No," Manuel whispers, breathing heavily, "*you* don't know. You don't know the fucking mess you got yourself into the day you touched my daughter."

Saïd is taken aback, his mouth half open.

"The day you got her pregnant and carried on being all cocky and didn't man up, you got yourself in the shit."

The penny finally drops. "*Céline?* Shit, I've never touched Céline! Never!"

The evidence is in his cry – he's telling the truth. Even Manuel, for all his anger, must realize that. But frankly, here and now, nobody gives a damn about the truth. It's much too late to worry about the truth.

"Sooner or later you'll admit it. I'm in no rush."

"I swear on Mecca, I've never touched Céline!"

"On Mecca? You think that'll save you?"

Saïd sniffs pathetically, muttering words to himself. The men prick up their ears but can't make out what he's saying. Manuel's face is switched off, pale. He grabs the bottle and takes a long swig. He proffers the bottle to Patrick but the other man declines with a gesture. Manuel puts the bottle back down, closes his eyes and clenches his fists. The kid is still droning faintly.

"Speak up, we can't hear anything."

Manuel's eyes are bloodshot, he's here to dispense justice, to take revenge, to make a clean sweep. He's getting his own back and won't let go.

"I've nothing to tell you, you sons of bitches."

The builder's foot cracks his shin. Saïd screams. Manuel is standing, sweating and breathing heavily. The tic in his cheek doesn't relent. He crosses his arms.

"We've got all night, you know."

Shoes. Shoes and clothes. An entire roomful. A room the size of a bedroom. Jo stands on tiptoe, in her swimsuit, wrapped in a towel she stole from the bathroom. There's a sailing boat on it, navy blue on a white background. From here, she can hear the music, trip hop, maybe Morcheeba, she's not sure. An old track, in any case, one she quite likes. With her free hand – the one not holding the towel tight above her breasts – she strokes the clothes as if they were arms.

"What are you doing?"

She jumps, caught in the act. She turns to Garance, gripping the towel from the bathroom.

"Nothing. I was looking."

"You can. If there's something you like, I can lend it to you."

"No, it's OK."

Jo almost pushes past her as she leaves the walk-in wardrobe.

"Have you seen my sister?"

"She's with Côme. Actually, he's – she's – I mean perhaps you'd better go to them. Côme can sometimes be a bit heavy-handed."

"What do you mean heavy-handed?"

Garance shrugs, looking embarrassed, but Jo isn't too worried: on the heavy-handed front, there's quite a distance before he's on the same level as Lucas or Enzo.

"I borrowed a towel."

"You did well. Shall we go down?"

Jo overtakes Garance on the stairs. She runs the flat of her hand down the banister, a kind of white, rounded wall, like in Greek houses. Under her bare feet, concrete slabs with ochre patterns, cool and dry, like the kind her father sometimes lays in houses that aren't his. She wants to touch everything here. From the walls, to the bookcases, to the lacquered body of the double bass she sees again in the lounge.

"Is it you who plays?"

"No, it's my sister. I play the piano, which is on the other side."

A vague gesture towards another part of the house and Garance leads Jo to the garden and the shrieking.

The pool is waiting for her, luring her, and she drops her towel on a deck chair, focusing on the blueness. No one's paying attention to her, not even the bathers messing about. The pool is large enough for her to slip in and swim without colliding with anybody. Jo lets herself sink, cutting herself off from the sounds. The thumping of the bass still echoes under the water, like a large choir, but she can no longer make out the details.

It's only after several minutes in the water that she finally worries about her sister.

When they were fifteen years old, Manuel remembers they used to like driving their scooters and squashing tree frogs on rainy days. They'd stream onto the small roads, numerous and suicidal, and make a happy popping sound under the scooter wheels. It's not raining tonight. The heat is crushing him but Manuel no longer feels anything. His fists come crashing into Saïd's face, which no longer looks like a face. He stares at the two bleeding slits that half open to look back at him. It's them he's addressing.

"Still nothing to say?"

He no longer expects an answer. All that's important is the tension in his fingers and in his stomach, which he thinks he'll soothe with every blow. Yes, it's doing him good. After all, it doesn't really matter who got his daughter pregnant any more. It's too late. He's had his chance, maybe or maybe not, but one thing's definite, and it's that he's wasted it. He's certain, convinced of it. All he has to do is remember the villa owner's look, that of his father-in-law, and of his wife. The absence of his father's look. So he's going to make the shitty little Arab who thinks he's superior, what with his car and his small-time wheeler-dealing, lower his eyes. That's all he's got left.

Patrick knocks back the rest of the whisky; he feels really awful, about to vomit. Powerless to put an end to what's going on, he steps back. His hands are shaking on the empty bottle.

"Now stop it, you're going to kill him."

Céline is still laughing. Even and especially when Côme slides his hands down her back. His mates are giving him sly looks, like, *You'll never dare: after all, she's pregnant, and she's sixteen.* But there's admiration in their eyes, challenges and all, *Côme does crazy stuff nobody else would dare.* There are even two girls watching, passively, from a distance.

Céline is laughing but declines with a vague gesture when the young man proffers her another drink – vodka this time, he's given up on beer, it's too slow at getting her drunk and then she keeps having to go and pee every fifteen minutes, which is a drag. He insists, and since she doesn't want to lose this smile, this attention that makes her feel beautiful, she takes the frozen glass.

"You'll see, it feels good, it's straight out of the freezer."

The little group surrounding them watches her drink greedily, the guy trying to give her a refill even though her head says no and her mouth grimaces.

"Stop, Côme, let go, you can see she doesn't want any more."

Céline is suddenly grateful, and holds no grudge about the previous drink – forgotten already. She smiles at him. He's a clever bastard. If she moves too much she's going to keel over, so she glances around for somewhere to sit. He anticipates this and catches her by the waist.

"Hey, this way, gorgeous, don't go fainting on us."

He drags her towards the house as the others watch, laughing with admiration and a vague sense of guilt. The little gang hesitates, waiting for a sign from Côme, a crack or an acknowledgement. So he eagerly obliges: with his free hand he pulls out his iPhone in camera mode and waves it like a treat over a dog's mouth. Not a word, just a greedy smile thrown at the gallery, a promise, and Céline doesn't react, too busy trying to walk in a straight line and savouring the pleasure of the arm around her, reassuring her.

Johanna follows her sister with her eyes. She hasn't witnessed the scene but can clearly see that Céline's plastered and Côme's a dickhead. Not heavy-handed like their mates at the technical high school, no. But still a dickhead, just a different variety.

By the time she heaves herself out of the water and fetches her towels, she's lost sight of them. Die Antwoord start singing "Enter the Ninja" and all the girls imitate the translucent performer, yelling, "I am your butterfly, I need your protection, be my samurai"; leaping, overexcited and half-naked. Somebody turns up the volume and the atmosphere heats up, bellies start to throb, bodies twist in a savage choreography, wet bodies, bare soles hitting the ground, narrow hips doing rounded, suggestive moves – there are no screwed-up uglies, amazing how well fed these kids are, as if they owned the world.

Jo searches with her eyes, zigzags amid the dancers, tempted, in spite of herself, to start contorting to "Banana Brain", which is now starting, even jerkier and crazier. The heat is everywhere in the muggy night, climbing up their bodies. Her heart starts beating faster and she doesn't know if it's because of the atmosphere, the music or because she's worried about Céline. Something's about to happen. Jo can feel it, like animals that sense disasters a few minutes before they happen. Not necessarily something bad, but something unpleasant she'd like to avoid. She goes back into the lounge, touches the wood of the double bass with her superstitious finger, ever so lightly, and wards off bad luck by drawing strength where she finds it, even in the most unlikely places.

Ignoring the upper floor, she instinctively looks for new rooms and remembers Garance's vague gesture when she mentioned a piano. Yes, the corridor at the end leads into another room with bay windows and a hell of a view over the Luberon, but it's too dark for her to notice, and besides, she's got other things to do. Behind the piano, a baby grand like in films, she makes out the couple on a cream sofa. Côme has switched on a small lamp so he doesn't miss a single detail. Céline is giggling, drunk, her T-shirt lifted to her armpits. Côme has removed her bra and her full breasts are bursting out in the soft light, above her belly. Jo freezes, surprised by the beauty of the scene. If that bastard wasn't filming it, she'd want to capture the moment. And that's what he's doing, although for a different reason. Even Côme's blonde hand, stroking, pinching and feeling, has something striking about it. Jo approaches and grabs his iPhone without taking her eyes off her sister. "Get dressed, we're off."

Côme turns and his face turns from realization to fear and then quickly to anger. "Shit, give that back to me!"

She scrolls through the photo gallery with her thumb and deletes as fast as she can. By the time he gets up and catches her by the wrist, she's erased the video and three pictures he's just taken of her sister. Jo deliberately drops the phone and it bounces softly on the rug. Too bad, she would have liked it to break, to split like an arched eyebrow under a fist.

Côme picks up his property and turns to Céline, who's pulled down her T-shirt, looking a little wild. "We weren't doing any harm, Jo."

"Not you."

Roles reversed, like so often. When is the day going to come when someone will protect *her*? Will worry about saving her from trouble, pull a sheet over her shoulders, hold her forehead while she's puking? Will that day ever come? Will she allow it? Maybe Saïd, but admittedly she doesn't really give him a chance.

"Come with me."

"Where?"

"We're going to get my clothes, and then we're out of here."

Céline looks down and picks up her bra from between the sofa cushions. She bites her lip and doesn't dare look at Côme. He grits his teeth, stares at the wall and shakes his head. He approaches Jo and stands in her way, without hostility. His hand swipes at his blonde lock of hair and lingers on the back of his neck. His eyes are almost liquid as he whispers to Jo, "You know, I wouldn't have shown it to the others."

"Like hell you wouldn't."

"I swear. It's what I was planning, but —"

"But what? You allegedly felt guilty, dickhead?"

He looks lost, and that's not usual for him. He suddenly looks like a child, or a much older man. "I don't know."

"*I* know."

"No, you're wrong. I think… I think I would have kept it to myself."

"Fucking idiot," Jo hisses, dragging Céline upstairs with her.

The stairs, the walk-in wardrobe, the bedrooms, the bathroom: she goes back the now familiar way. She puts on her
clothes, rolls up her swimsuit in a plastic bag. A hollow
rage tenses her jaw, preventing her from crying. She dives
into the walk-in wardrobe, grabs a large travel bag made of
glossy leather, of an elegance that's alien to her. Under the
slightly dazed eyes of Céline, Jo mechanically tears down
the clothes that she can get her hands on that are softest
to the touch and stuffs them into the bag.

"You're crazy," Céline tries to say, regaining her stupid
drunk smile, a small flicker of greed lighting up her eyes.

She bends down to pick up a pair of shoes and adds it to
the loot. Then another and then – why not, while they're
at it? – a jacket.

Bag firmly closed, they rush down the stairs. At the
bottom of the steps, Jo stops her sister and shoves the bag
into her arms. "Wait here."

She zigzags between the others, who've spread into the
corridor, making her way amid the laughter to the kitchen,
where she grabs a bottle of champagne and a box of pizza.
Back to Céline, she motions her to the exit with a nod. A
techno cover of Aretha Franklin accompanies their escape.

Think, think, think, let your mind go, let yourself be free.

They don't come across either Garance or Côme. They
don't look at anybody.

And nobody looks at them.

Manuel has stopped punching. His fists are red, his head
drenched in sweat. He seems to be trying to snap out of it,
but it's a long process. He feels empty inside, as though a
huge blankness has eaten his insides, and he can't even feel

his own breathing, though he can hear it, loud and raspy, panting with terror. It seems to be filling the whole space of the garage. Time is passing through his throaty breathing and his irregular heartbeat.

"Fuck, Manuel…" That's all Patrick manages to say, but Manuel doesn't answer. He's not even sure he can hear him. So he repeats, "Fuck, Manuel. Fuck. Fuck. Is he…? Fuck. Oh, fuck." Patrick still isn't sure. He's telling himself maybe it's going to be all right. "It's going to be all right," he says out loud. Softly, at first, just to himself, then to his motionless friend. "It's going to be all right. Fuck, fuck, fuck. It's going to be all right." He's comforted by his own voice, even if it's talking rubbish. His hoarse voice, in this garage shiny with humid heat, has the fleshy tone of great tragedies, of empty promises. "It's going to be all right."

Check, first. Yes, but the blood – he doesn't want to get his hands sticky, he's already thinking police – ballistics – murder – prison. He must think for the both of them. He owes him that much, to this tall, wild guy who's still out of breath from punching so hard and so long. Taking over, Patrick puts his fingers on Saïd's neck in spite of the blood. The weight of the broken jaw on his hand makes him want to vomit. The silence under the skin confirms what he already knows; you don't survive this kind of beating.

"Don't move. I'll get a tarpaulin."

Patrick looks around and finds one of those transparent sheets that protect the parquet when walls are being repainted. He thinks technique and effectiveness. He unrolls a fair amount on the concrete floor of the garage. He starts cutting into the insulating tape at the wrists with his Leatherman, taking care not to damage the Voltaire armchair, but he's already thinking about the best way of getting rid of it.

Frozen, Manuel still hasn't stirred, and isn't even trying to wipe the sweat running down his neck, bathing the back of it.

"You have to help me now." Patrick has grabbed Saïd bodily – too bad about the blood – and is trying to push him onto the tarpaulin. He's struggling. "Fuck, Manuel! Help me…"

Manuel finally looks at his friend and clicks into motion, like a large obedient puppet. Together, they lay the limp body on the plastic sheet. Patrick holds the head so it doesn't knock against the ground and lays it down gently, letting his fingers slide behind the curly-haired neck – a living man's consideration, an excuse. He's the one who folds the tarpaulin over the pulped face, the red swellings, the twisted body. He wonders whether he should empty his pockets and check … check what?

"Manuel, the insulating tape, next to you."

He obeys, unrolls the tape and crouches to secure the sheet around the body.

"Wait."

Manuel stands up, looks like he's thinking again, and lights a cigarette. Between them, Saïd's body is lying under the thick plastic and smudges of blood are sticking to the opaque grey. Manuel is thinking about the series he sometimes watched with Séverine in the evenings, a series in which the cops always find the culprit. It's no longer a tic that's making his face twitch but a violent trembling that seizes his body. He shakes his head like a stubborn animal.

"What are we doing?"

Patrick pretends not to understand, opens his arms and shrugs, as if to say *Have you got a better idea?*

Manuel walks across the garage, his back to the scene, then comes back. He sniffs and finally wipes the trails of sweat with his T-shirt. He crushes his cigarette in a jar of turpentine and persuades himself that he doesn't have a choice. He takes a deep breath. "The decorative pond."

The two men no longer look at each other. They won't speak any more. Right now, they must act quickly and efficiently. Their minds are working overtime; they get down to work.

They've known many summer nights. Bright and warm, seldom dark – there are many stars the night before a glorious day. This one's very light, with a three-quarter moon, a peace interrupted only by the rustling of cicadas further away. And the screeching of an eagle owl at regular intervals. Jo counts between each cry, like between a flash of lightning and its rumble. They walk on the edge of the road and step into a ditch whenever a car drives by.

"It's stupid to hide like that. We'd better hitch a ride."

"Not yet."

"Did you see how far it is? I'm not walking all the way home, I'm warning you."

"Don't worry. Come with me for now."

Johanna is still holding the box with the pizza and the bottle of champagne; she takes a narrow path that goes uphill and her sister follows her. They walk for a few minutes but Céline gets breathless, so Jo gives her the pizza and grabs the bag, which is heavier.

"Remember this place?"

"Isn't it where Anthony used to throw rocks at the cars?"

"Yeah, and he wasn't the only one."

"All right, all right, I did it once —"

"Why is it that every time a guy does something insane, you do it with him?"

Céline chuckles, and Jo imitates her.

"It was after the school fete, the one where we had to dress up as Provençales."

"Don't remind me."

"Scary…"

They settle on a huge, flat rock – they call it the Butter Rock around here, nobody knows why. It overhangs the valley, and the road runs right beneath it. Jo uncorks the champagne. The pop echoes around her.

"Actually, good thing our parents didn't come and see us. No pictures —"

"Oh, but you looked so cute with your little lace bonnet."

"Shut up. You didn't look much better."

They laugh. Some champagne has spilled on Jo's legs. She drinks and grimaces. "It doesn't even taste nice. I should have got a beer instead."

Céline opens the box with the pizza and this time she's so hungry, she starts wolfing it down. She's passed the fifth month and doesn't get nauseous any more. Of course, she's a bit too drunk tonight, but the pizza fills a gap and she seems to be keeping it down. The thing stirs a little, she's been feeling it over the past few days. For the time being, she still pretends she doesn't really know. She leans towards Jo and rubs her head against her like a cat. "Thanks." And since Jo lifts an eyebrow, puzzled, she adds, "For earlier on."

They won't mention it again, enough said as it is. The bag is lying at Johanna's feet, and the champagne gets drunk. They plunge into silence the way they get into the water of a pool: suddenly, simultaneously and palpably. Alone and yet together. It can last a long time and it's precious, even if they don't know that yet. They'll get back home later, there are always cars driving past on a Saturday night, even here, in the armpit of the world, in this rich tourist village they know only too well.

Céline wriggles her varnished toes in her high-heeled sandals, then slips the straps off and puts the soles of her feet on the rock. It's not as cold as she would have imagined. She's drunk but feeling good. Then, in the silence, her eyes fixed on her toes, Céline allows herself to think about *him*.

It had started last summer. Or maybe earlier. Maybe she'd always harboured the childish hope that he'd see her as a woman. Maybe it was even for his sake that she'd made herself more giggly and exercised her power of attraction ruthlessly. The Lucases and the others were just practice runs, guinea pigs so she'd be ready for a man, a real man. One who'd know everything she thought she knew nothing about.

Céline would drive boys nuts, but inside she was always dreaming of old-fashioned romantic scenes, sunsets on the beach like the ones decorating her bedroom walls. They bragged to one another, told their mates. She'd do things, true, quite a few things in fact; a load of things other girls didn't really do, even the older ones who weren't virgins any more. That's why she had the kind of reputation only villagers can pin on you.

Patrick had always touched her, to make her laugh, to mess around. She was like a niece, the child he'd never had. When had that changed? When had it become an obsession, a problem or a solution? For Céline, the turmoil had been there so long, she couldn't have said when exactly. She didn't like to think about those hours at the end of her childhood when she'd look in the bathroom mirror and watch her breasts grow. She preferred to think about Patrick's hands caressing them as though they were the perfect size.

But there was one recollection, more vivid than the others, that she associated with the beginning of this whole thing, one she would sometimes think about with a kind of embarrassed excitement, the kind that increased her desire.

They'd all gone to Salin-de-Giraud, a picnic in the bed of the pick-up truck. Patrick and Valérie had taken the girls with them, in the back of their Peugeot 205. The pick-up was behind them, with Manuel and Séverine in the cabin. Once they'd left the main roads, they'd parked by the wayside; Patrick, Céline and Jo had climbed into the back of the truck, while Séverine had joined Valérie in the small car. Céline remembered the road like a loud scream, a gale in their faces, shrieking with laughter, laughing like idiots. Standing up, clinging to the crossbar above the cabin, they tackled the road head-on, and Manuel had fun swerving suddenly to throw them off balance. It was a bit stupid and dangerous, but funny. Patrick had glued himself to Céline, his belly against her buttocks, an arm around her waist to stop her from falling over. In Céline's memory, there were herds of dark bulls along the road, and the first pink flamingoes had made them giggle overexcitedly. Family outings, or with friends of their parents, didn't happen very often. At the weekend, the men would do their odd jobs and the women would go shopping. The girls would veg out in front of the TV or go and smoke in the fields with their village mates. Weekends would drag from doing nothing, but were always too short despite their complaining about monumental boredom. She didn't remember their ever having gone further than Salin-de-Giraud at any point. She's never even taken the train, except once to go to Avignon with her class in year nine; a visit to the Pope's Palace and the Petit Palais museum, and she was bored to death among the badly proportioned religious paintings.

The bodywork had been quivering under her feet and a cool wind had accompanied this exceptional, luminous Saturday. Patrick's erection against her buttocks had been at once a shock and a relief – a confirmation. Jo didn't see anything, too filled with wonder at the flamingoes in flight, the bulky beauty of the bulls, her senses in turmoil because of the smell of iodine as they approached the salt pans. They had carried on laughing, accomplices of the forbidden, carriers of a huge, silent secret. They knew. It was now just a matter of time and opportunity. Céline couldn't care less if the age difference was a problem for Patrick, or the fact that she was his best friend's daughter and only fifteen years old. In time, she would even realize that this side of things had made it more enticing. A very typical emotion, as if being desired by a man could turn all young girls into women. Make up for their naivety and their silly little-girl dreams. She'd arched her back slightly. She had nothing with which to compare the excitement that overwhelmed her at that moment. A combination of terror and absolute joy. It was new, it was a world.

On the beach, Patrick had behaved as usual, competing with corny jokes with his friend Manuel, holding Valérie, running after Jo or Céline to splash them, like an uncle playing at being an imaginary monster. Céline had even ended up doubting herself.

On their way back, he had sat behind the wheel of the 205. Valérie was scratching the sand from her ankles and trying to get Jo and Céline, silent and slumped on the back seat, to talk. Despite her efforts, she'd never managed to establish a very warm bond with them even when they were little.

At one point, Patrick had run over a coypu, killed the animal on the spot and stained the road with blood. The girls had screamed in disgust.

"What are you thinking about?"

"Nothing."

"Right. My foot…"

"Perhaps, instead of your foot, you'd better start using your pussy a little more."

Jo smiles in the night and thinks about Saïd's naked chest, about the warmth in the bathroom, and the sickening smell of ether.

Her smile broadens and she hands the bottle to her sister – might as well.

"Don't worry, it'll happen."

The Decorative Pond

The guys whistle with admiration. Even Gypsy shows respect after seeing how much the work has progressed.

"Did you two do this?"

"Yeah, we stayed behind last night to get ahead," Patrick explains. "We made the cast and laid the welded wire mesh."

"And the concrete?"

"We got here early this morning and poured it into the mould."

The guys are blown away, almost sheepish for having made a fuss yesterday. A team leader who works harder than his men deserves respect. They give Manuel sly looks and shake their heads.

"She can christen it at her daughter's wedding," one of the men says, laughing.

"She'll still have to wait a week for it to be completely dry," Patrick says, "but it should be OK. She's not going to piss us off."

The team is reunited before the enemy.

Manuel says nothing. At the top of his large, gladiator's body, his head is nodding gently from tiredness and his tic hasn't stopped, it's got worse, in fact: his cheek twitches involuntarily under his sunglasses. His wrecked hands are stuffed inside the pockets of his jacket, even though it's actually too hot to be wearing one. He rubs his fingers together, bits of concrete crumbling against the fabric. His sore knuckles, chafed to the blood, remind him he's alive.

He replays bits of the night on a loop. He buries the early part: too dark, too alcoholic, and besides, it'll surface soon enough. For now, he's rethinking the careful finishing stages of the decorative pond. First the bed of gravel, the body lying at the bottom, in a semicircle, and on top of it the scrap iron they carried together. And then the fifteen or so inches of cement poured over that, twenty for good measure, just to make sure, to be safe. They worked quickly, each and every movement calculated, efficient. It wasn't just about a couple of hounded guys; they were – they thought – far removed from genre movies. In fact, preparing the cement in the middle of the night and fussing over the mixer gave them respite. Not thinking and just moving their bodies in familiar gestures. They didn't look at each other.

By the time the sun rose on their filthy, shattered bodies and empty eyes, they'd finished. The little Voltaire armchair had its legs sawn off and its back broken; it's lying in pieces under an old hunting parka and gnarled vine stocks in the bed of the pick-up truck. It'll have to wait a while: leaves get burnt in the late autumn, sometimes even in the winter.

The concrete has now set enough for them to draw breath. And for hell to begin.

Turning his back on his team, Manuel takes out a cigarette and lights it in the cup of his hands as if the mistral was sweeping over everything. But there's not even a breath of air on the hill – nothing but light, omnipresent heat and blueness.

Even in Our Own Backyard

Even though Jo is surprised not to see Saïd in the days following Garance's party, she's not really worried. It's summer, there's that heavy bag of clothes at the end of her bed and Garance trying to call her, but she won't answer. The prospect of term starting at the lycée and the languor of an August that stretches out, clammy. It's only when the gendarmes turn up at the housing development that things start to stir and questions arise.

They're not exactly frantic in the beginning. Saïd's mother has reported him missing and since he's over eighteen, the police are almost doing her a favour by looking into it. So many people go missing every year, go far away and are forgotten. But the police ask questions anyway. They don't enquire about his timetable the day he disappeared; they're strange questions, about Saïd's childhood, who he kept company with.

But there's not much to say. Saïd's never caused any trouble. A local boy who attended the same school as all the other kids here. Collège Paul Gauthier in Cavaillon, Lycée Dumas – the technical, not the general one. A kid who hung around the same places as the kids of the farmers, the builders and the gendarmes. He went through the crappy fetes, the winter lottery, climbed the chateau ruins – above Fontaine-de-Vaucluse – on a day trip with the school sporting union. He's smoked a few joints, loitered in the village square, flirted clumsily with girls, kicked the same ball as the others at the Taillades football club – better than the Imberts one, and the trainer liked him. In year eight he even went out with Carole, the Cabrières grocer's daughter. Moreover, when they question the grocer, he is only too happy to tell them what he thinks of Arabs sniffing around his daughter, and this one in particular. He's bound to have left to do jihad, the way he'd look at pork chops on the barbecue. Besides, a man who vanishes like that, so unexpectedly, that's weird, isn't it?

So all of a sudden there's a bit of a commotion, a surge in energy, a paradoxical excitement at the thought that here, too, they have Arabs who go to Syria. Because the gendarmes already have their theory and would quite like to have it confirmed. It creates a kind of self-conscious joy, helps people talk freely. Saïd's mother knows he would never have done this, but all mothers say that, don't they?

So the police take over from the gendarmes and question more closely, and go into houses that are more welcoming than when it's about a tractor being stolen, poaching, or the rape of a local girl. People offer a drink, sometimes two, and bring out the pistachios.

I've always wondered. And theory becomes truth. The grocery shop is always crowded despite the two-euros-a-pound aubergines and the owner's inability to give the correct change. There's much talk amid the market stalls, people remember things, and what they don't know, they make up. An anxious excitement, the pleasure of self-importance at being at the heart of things. *Good God, even in our own backyard.* Basically, everybody feels they finally exist.

Saïd's mother no longer goes out, and her sisters keep their heads down when they go shopping in the village.

"It's so stupid," Jo grumbles all day long. "They're crazy."

"You don't know that," her mother replies. She's been going to the grocer's quite a lot the past few days.

Her father doesn't say anything. Her father doesn't say anything any more, anyway, just works and comes home late. He's started on a new building site in Roussillon. When he gets back, he drinks quite a few beers then collapses in a heap on his side of the bed.

As for Céline, she's still feeding the seasonal workers with her grandmother, sits down more often, and carries fewer bottles. The guys are sweet, they help her, and also wonder about Saïd's disappearance.

One evening, Saïd's mother pops round, in tears. She looks into Manuel's eyes as he stands in the garden, a halo of mosquitoes around him under the outdoor light. He thinks about Saïd, about the broken body beneath the cubic feet of cement. He thinks about it as though it had nothing to do with him and feels sorry for the dishevelled woman who looks at him, sniffing. Then a pang of shame stabs him in the stomach. He coughs and looks away.

When the police come to the house, they sit on the lemon-yellow sofa and don't beat about the bush. Did Johanna and Céline know him well? Did Saïd ever talk about religion, advocate purity, denounce Western decadence?

Jo gets the feeling they're using words they don't entirely understand, as if they've just learned them. But Jo's a pain. She shakes her head and mocks them. "Western decadence? No, he drinks Coke, likes girls and has never made any remarks about Céline's outfits... And yet there are guys here who don't hold back."

Séverine puckers her lips. She's sitting opposite them, cross-legged, earnest. "You can never really tell, you know. He was working for my parents and all of a sudden he's gone... Goes to show you can never really trust them, right?"

Jo gets worked up. "*Them?* Who do you mean exactly?"

Her mother's usually not as fucking stupid as her father about these things.

"Let your mother say what she has to say, Mademoiselle. We're here to listen to everyone."

The policeman listens to Séverine's remarks. He probably finds her attractive and sympathizes with her concerns; he, too, has a daughter and he wouldn't want her to —

"What was the nature of your relationship with him?" the second policeman suddenly asks Jo and Céline, interrupting their mother's babbling laced with everyday racism.

"We've been friends since school," Jo replies. "Me more than Céline."

Céline nods, backing her sister's statement. "Yes, I like him, but he's particularly into Jo."

"You're such a bitch."

"What? It's true, Saïd's been in love with you for years. The guy would do anything for you, drives his car six miles to do you a favour, always at your beck and call whenever you need him. I can't think of many people who'd do that."

Now this seems to interest the police, and they immediately turn to Jo. "Mademoiselle, has he given you presents?"

She laughs, embarrassed by the *Mademoiselle.* "Not many, he hasn't got much money. But when we were little, he made me things. Mangas he'd draw himself and staple in the middle." She makes a gesture with her hands, mimicking a book with pages you can turn, and stops.

"What do you do with him?"

173

"What do you mean?"

The one who started this doesn't take his eyes off Johanna but doesn't go into detail, while the other one looks embarrassed – maybe he's putting it on to reassure the parents.

"Well, we go to the river, we hang out. I mean, this year we haven't been to the river, he was working too hard, doing stuff."

"What stuff?"

"I don't know, working, seeing his mates, usual stuff. Besides, I haven't been around much."

"Where have you been?"

"In Avignon, at the festival. But he drove me there when I needed it and came to pick me up. When I had difficulty with buses." She smiles at her sister. It's true that Saïd's reliable.

Séverine intervenes. "Wait, what's all these questions? My daughters haven't done anything. You're interrogating them as if they've done something wrong."

"Not at all, they haven't done anything wrong. We're just trying to get a clearer picture."

His colleague smiles at Manuel, seeking an ally.

Manuel can't understand how things could have escaped him to this point. He feels a void inside, as painful as a fall from a great height. He goes to fetch a beer from the fridge, offers one to the policemen, who decline with a gesture. Séverine, however, demands a beer.

"Are you a little more than friends … Johanna?" the first policeman insists.

"What's the difference?"

Jo stands up, tense. She's sorry for having given away a piece of her friend, and has the impression everything she says will be soiled and turned into something else.

"Listen, Johanna, you wouldn't want to be responsible for something serious, would you?"

The policeman has taken on a deep voice to say that, and glances at the television that's on, broadcasting the news on a loop. Nothing to do with the subject – the reporters are talking about the imminent presidential elections. But everybody understands very well what he's driving at. Her parents' presence is making Jo angry; this confession session is stripping her naked and she hates strangers calling her by her first name.

"We've been going out since January, but we haven't done anything."

Silence; the policeman smiles at her warmly. "Thank you, Johanna, thank you very much."

The pair's gratitude isn't earth-shattering. As soon as they've left and said goodbye to everybody, the two teenagers shut themselves in their room. Séverine drinks her beer in small sips, her legs folded under her in the armchair.

The police won't be back; they've got scraps of information, the bare bones of a personality, dozens of paranoid bits of gossip, but no evidence and no truth. Saïd's file will be added to others, while the entire region will build a myth around the young man.

Manuel wishes he hadn't heard anything, doesn't want to know. What's the point of knowing all this now? It sounds like childish play, clumsy kindness and patience – that's not what he wanted to hear. The gap is too wide between the boy described by his daughters and the grown, arrogant man he took revenge on. Through totally insane mental gymnastics, he tells himself that the police are right, that Saïd kept his cards close to his chest, that he must have gone to Syria or joined a terrorist cell. And even if he hasn't, he could have. This description would justify his hatred, but he doesn't believe it for a second. Realizing he'll never be bothered again, Manuel feels immense relief and at the same time a terrible weight on his solar plexus; he instinctively knows he's going to have to live with it now. He tells himself that the lives of some men aren't worth much. Himself included, even though he's not dead.

How he wishes his mother was still around.

Old Things

Céline doesn't like her old primary school teacher. She didn't like her when she was a child, either. She had that way of talking, so kind and sweet that it made Céline cringe. A way of cocking her head to the side with a sullen pout, ridiculous on the face of a grown-up woman, to show a naughty child that she was very disappointed. She had to put up with her for several years at primary school, as the teacher changed classes at the same time as her; a curse that repeated itself every year until high school. She wasn't nasty, quite the opposite, but although unable to pinpoint it exactly, Céline sensed in her look and body language a contempt that seeped through that fake kindness. Like when she'd sigh and shake her head when some children told others about a film they'd watched the night before and which they obviously shouldn't have. Or like when they'd unwrap their packed snacks after class: fizzy drinks and cookies and a family-size bag of tortilla chips or something. Because she wasn't the only one in the village and at school to be the butt of this contempt. There were many parents in the area who'd let their kids grow wild, without a timetable, staying up late to watch the box. But that bitch couldn't possibly understand. She'd moved here for the sun and the stone-clad walls, the traditional markets and the ever-so-charming accent.

Sometimes, Céline would picture secret things she knew she couldn't admit to: the teacher being shot against the green blackboard, just like the way she'd seen in a war film with her father, seeing the same bullets hitting her large breasts under the patterned dresses. Jo had had a better deal: she'd only got her for one year, when Céline was in year seven. And Jo could keep people at arm's length, while Céline would wallow in her resentment.

She looks old now. She retired some time ago, and Céline is always surprised to see that she's still alive whenever she bumps into her – inevitably while shopping or in the village.

Her mother didn't give her a choice this morning: the shopping chore, and Céline didn't dare refuse – at the moment she's trying to be positive, would like to send everybody to hell and yet also longs for a hug that would allow her to go back to being a child. And so mother and daughter are criss-crossing the Intermarché, each with a wheeled trolley and part of the list in her head. When she sees the teacher a few feet away, shopping trolley full, thin body and large chest resting on the handle, short-sighted eyes peering at the health-food shelf, Céline speeds up to find her mother, as if she could protect her from the old nutcase. As if her mother had ever protected her from anything at all. She skedaddles, hoping the old woman hasn't seen her, but she's already waving and forcing her limp, condescending presence on her.

"Céline!"

The girl reluctantly turns around.

Squashing her chest against the shopping trolley to move forward, the old woman moves quickly enough to come level with Céline, who doesn't react and declines a handshake and an unwelcome kiss.

"So, darling, how are you? I heard about…"

Her smile is hungry for new information, her eyes glued to the girl's belly. Céline wonders how the old bitch found out. She curses the indiscretion and speedy effect of inappropriate chatter, resolves not to tell her anything, not let anything on about what she's feeling. She manages it quite well at the beginning, with her perennial insolent pout verging on a smile, her glorious mascara and dark eyelids.

The retired teacher studies her former pupil, now grown up, a woman, *but still a bad sort*, she thinks. "Are you pleased?"

Céline can't help frowning slightly with an expression of incomprehension, so the teacher lets out a self-conscious little laugh, suddenly aware of her futile question. "I mean, is everything going well?"

Céline shrugs. She hesitates for a second, looks at the old woman intently and remembers her childhood, so recent. She doesn't reply.

Despite the girl's silence, the woman's gaze slides to her trolley and assesses inquisitively the choice of goods, then travels back to her belly. Céline thinks about the little thing inside her.

"What are you going to do afterwards?"

Coming from the teacher's mouth, it doesn't sound like when Jo said it. Céline shrugs again, still says nothing.

"And the father?"

The woman's gaze grows more insistent, and sheds some of its benevolence. Her smile remains fixed, like that of dolls in horror films, Céline thinks. She looks around; the other customers aren't paying attention to them. Céline feels as though the world has taken on a menacing dimension and could swallow her whole, something she's never felt before. She puts a hand on her belly. Pity suddenly appears on the woman's face, a revolting pity that extends to the child. The teenager could scratch her eyes out. And, for the first time since she found out she's pregnant, Céline wants to protect the baby growing inside her. She can't put it into words, it's beyond her, and she wants to find her mother.

"My mother's waiting for me." Céline rouses herself, commands her legs to resume their course, to extricate themselves from this face-to-face.

"Wait! If you need anything at all —"

"I don't need anything. And nobody. Fuck you!"

The teacher is suddenly upright, frozen in her astonishment, offended and stuttering.

Céline pushes her trolley in front of her like a shield or a ram to smash enemy doors down. She finishes her shopping quickly, throwing items into her trolley with methodical rage. She reaches the tills out of breath, as tense as a cornered animal, her back rippling with haste. Her mother is already in the queue and looks at her blankly, but Céline smiles at her.

One Day, on La Rambla

"Will you go to Spain for me?"

"Yes, Grandpa."

"Go to La Rambla, Jojo, it's so beautiful, you'll see. There's always people dancing there. And at the very end, almost at the harbour, there are stone lions. Will you go and see them?"

"Yes, Grandpa."

"Say hello to them from me."

"Yes."

"My father was very proud, Jojo. You're like him, you know. He always had that look, like you, always a little angry, on alert, as if somebody was about to take something away from him that he cared about. I remember he used to tell me about when he arrived at the Argèles camp, the stagnant water, and his sister getting ill. She died there, you know, my aunt. I never met her... Her name was Pepita, and she survived the war to then die in France because of dirty water, imagine that?"

Jo smiles at her grandfather; she knows the story but is quite happy to hear it again. It's better than silence. It's better than this wet chewing sound he makes when he struggles to breathe, and the nasal vibration, the hiccups – his entire body falling apart.

"Go and have a drink on the Plaza de España. And in the Carrer de Tarragona, I remember there's a bar my father took me to when he first went back there, after Franco's death. And the Horta garden…"

The old man's wild eyes are staring at the wall, he gets lost in the Parc del Laberint d'Horta, sees his father's face at the same age as he is now, just before his death, and that of Franco being eaten by stone lions.

"Yes, Grandad."

"Wait, I forgot what it's called. I'll remember it in a second – a bar where they do the most amazing tapas."

Jo is tired. She can't understand why Saïd isn't contacting her. OK, so he's gone, but why didn't he say anything to her? She's full of questions that lead her nowhere.

"Do you want to take a stroll somewhere else? I can push your wheelchair down the corridors. Or go downstairs."

The hospital garden is not very large, but it does have a couple of leafy hedges and enough greenery to make you believe in rebirth, in spring and that kind of crap. And then there are a few birds. She'd rather that than this room where she knows every corner, the corridors with the beige linoleum, the plastic plants – or sometimes real ones, donated by a family, after a patient dies.

"No, I'm tired, and besides, it's teatime soon."

Jo swallows; she finds it hard. Her grandfather gives off a stale, rancid smell, a smell of old fridge and cologne gone off. She tries to imagine what she'd be thinking if she had only a few months left to live – all she can find is fear, and naive, desperate begging.

Johanna has never been anywhere. Not even on school trips, because her parents wouldn't pay. She thinks about Spain, about couples dancing the Argentine tango on La Rambla, welded by the rhythm. Her grandfather is giving her something tangible, the name of a station, the destination of a possible escape, someday, eventually – an invaluable gift. The old man doesn't know it. He's fidgeting in his wheelchair, impatient to munch on his Petit Lu cookies softened in stewed fruit. Spoon-fed by Chloé or perhaps Justine, the pretty blonde with her hair cut low across her forehead who speaks a little loudly. And who laughs at his jokes when he has the courage to tell some. He knows them all by their first names. And yet usually there's not much time to get acquainted in palliative care. He's been here a long time.

"How's your father?"

"Hasn't he been to see you these past few days?"

"Yes."

"And?"

"He said he was made foreman at his last building site." The old man's face wrinkles in a smile. There's a beautiful light in his dying eyes. "I'm proud of him."

"Did you tell him?"

He doesn't answer and suddenly starts looking around the wheelchair for an invisible object. His eyes grow hollow and he suddenly seems lost.

"What's happened to your grandmother? She said she'd be back straight away."

Jo bites at a fingernail. She feels like crying.

"Why isn't she back, Jojo? She said she wouldn't be long."

The girl stands up. "She has to talk to Papa, don't worry. I'll go and tell her to come here."

"Thank you, *gatito. Besame.*"

Jo rummages through her bag, pulls out a copy of *L'Humanité* and puts it down next to the bed, then bends over the old man and kisses his wrinkles. She didn't like to when she was a child. Ever since he's been declining, she always tells herself that perhaps this is the last time she'll kiss him. By extension, she tells herself this about many other things, even the ones she does for the first time. It's a bit morbid, but deserves consideration.

Summer Rain

At fifteen, you're not supposed to skip school to go and pick grapes – but after that summer, nobody's thought of imposing anything at all on Jo. So she joins the farmworkers for a back-breaking job over the vines. Because that's where she feels like being, and the lycée can wait a week. She has to put aside some cash now she has a project; the harvest provides life-saving physical exhaustion, the enjoyment of gestures repeated ad infinitum. There isn't much hand-harvesting in the area any more, but her grandparents have preserved the habit. A billhook in hand, she cuts and progresses along every row with the energy of an escape, and fills her bucket. She feels a peaceful satisfaction. Every so often she looks up and leans back, hands on her lower back. At the ten o'clock break, she curls her fingers, sticky from grape juice, around a cup of coffee, her back already cracking from all the bending, like the others. She likes these rituals, the eye contact with the other pickers, the complicity with those who get exhausted together and drink from the same feeding bottle.

As for Céline, she carts her big belly between the workers and their grandparents' kitchen. She looks like she's been doing this all her life.

The afternoon isn't over but large, dark clouds gather over the hill: the impending thunderstorm has apocalyptic colours. It's still hot when the first drops, sonorous and fat, start falling on the leaves, the soil and the pickers' backs.

"Let's take shelter!" the old Kabylian shouts, followed by the rest of the group.

The thunderstorm is too heavy to stay out in. These downpours are like showers, they know them well: might as well take shelter and wait for it to pass. Pulling their shirts or jackets over their heads, they run for the protection of the awning, enjoying the escape, already taking out their packets of cigarettes. They snort like animals, hand around a lighter, complain for the sake of it.

"Where are you going?" a worker asks Jo when she leaves the shelter.

"I need to pee."

"Can't you wait for it to calm down?"

"No, besides, I like the rain."

In fact, it's more than that: Jo is fascinated by the thunderstorm, and she's already running through the groves to distance herself from the others and take advantage of the rain.

Jo looks like a twig. She's kept the golden tint of the summer and her skin glows despite the grey-green that casts a shadow over the valley and colours the sky. Golden and, all things considered, wild rather than fierce. In large strides on her long legs, she cuts across the paths through the copses like an animal. The soil smells so strong that she feels an exquisite unease – as if treading on a body. She'd like to take off her shoes, heel-sole-toes in the moss, the mud, the uneven curve of the white rocks. She'd like to but doesn't dare yet. It'll come.

For now she runs, gets out of breath, breathes noisily, then stops, hands on her knees, and catches her breath with her head down. She's come quite a long way. She straightens up and removes her T-shirt, already drenched, and offers her torso and face to the sky. The rain hammers on her shoulders, her forehead, runs in gullies down her head, the small of her back, between her breasts. And yet she doesn't shiver once. The warmth comes from inside, making her euphoric. And if she does feel the rain running inside her, then it's still a full, refreshing sensation. She's not cold.

She hasn't seen Garance again. Nor Côme. Nor any of them. The bag is still in her room; Céline wanted to try the jacket on, but Jo exercised a veto: nobody's going to touch the contents of the bag. Since her fierce opposition seemed like a strange fixation, Céline gave up. She looked her sister deep in her left eye, shook her head, and said, *you're a bitch.*

Jo asked Saïd's friends, the ones in the Docteur Ayme neighbourhood, if they'd seen him again, but nobody knew anything. The two mates who were going to join him clearly shut their mouths immediately, used to the police constantly harassing them. Some of them were questioned by the police, but then nothing had happened. The guys would shrug, annoyed that Saïd hadn't let them in on his secret, but since he'd started hanging around antique dealers, he'd got a bit cocky. So Jo then also went to ask questions around the second-hand market in Isle-sur-la-Sorgue, but the old thieves with dandy airs didn't know anything either. The car remained parked outside the house for a while but then disappeared. His father must have sold it. His mother holds back her tears whenever the girls drop by. As a result, the girls no longer drop by that often. But Jo works near her in the vineyard.

She now takes off her shoes, leaving her damp socks scrunched up at the bottom of her sneakers. Then her jeans, which stick to her thighs. She staggers a little – the moisture has made the fabric clingy – but she pulls them off, the way an insect tears off its skin, and throws them inside out onto the strongly fragrant, wild mint that has taken over part of the ground.

Strange, how you get used to everything. Jo wouldn't have thought that Saïd's absence would become a part of her life. He's always been there, and yet she accepts his disappearance with a subtle resentment, as if he'd left to spite her. This creates a void, a pain of abandonment that makes the colours of her life more intense. She pictures him settling, alone, in a foreign country; she sees him walking down unfamiliar streets, glorified by having dared to take this step. Sometimes, she thinks he simply fell into a ditch and died of exposure, but this theory doesn't stick. She prefers the other version, the one where he's strolling around a foreign city in his Ray-Bans; then he thinks about her and perhaps feels sorry for abandoning her here. She, too, is going to leave. She's sure of it now.

The rain suddenly intensifies, buries her in the mud up to her ankles, and the downpour breaks up the landscape, cutting her off from the rest of the world. She can't see further than five yards; in any case, it's raining so hard she has to close her eyes. The rain drums on her body, stings her skin and runs down it, like caresses after blows. This goes on for a few minutes or much longer, a dance with very few moves. Then Johanna throws her head back and lets out a throaty, animal-like scream that's neither a moan nor a call but a little of both, a scream that extends her, hoarse and euphoric. But when she runs out of breath and falls quiet, there's another scream that responds to her silence; several screams, in fact, that blend with the noise of the rain and come from her grandparents' house. She thinks she can even hear her name.

Are they worried about her? Or is it something else?

The magic has gone: the strange trance, with her feet in the mud, suddenly seems out of place and embarrassing. She gets dressed. The jeans stick and she has trouble putting them on; she doesn't bother with the socks, and sprints barefoot to the house, a shoe in each hand.

Despite the rain, there's a commotion beneath the linden tree.

Her sister, bent double, is letting out little moans, while her grandmother is panicking over her phone. The workers are yelling, each giving advice on the next step to take.

"We can take my car!" Pascal shouts over the melee, but the old woman gestures at him to keep quiet – she's trying unsuccessfully to get through to her daughter or her son-in-law on the phone.

Jo counts in her head. *Six months isn't long; OK, it might be seven, but that still doesn't make nine.*

Pascal runs to his old Peugeot, parked further down the path. He starts the engine and drives up to the linden tree. The others make way and Céline gets in the back. Just as her grandmother is about to sit in the passenger seat, Jo rushes to the car and plants herself in front of the door.

"I'll go, Grandma. You can stay here."

The old woman looks at Jo's bare feet, covered in mud, at her body drenched by the downpour. She removes her woollen cardigan and puts it over her shoulders.

"Go. I'll try and tell your mother."

"And my father."

"And your father."

Céline cries out in pain, curled up on the back seat.

"Go, hurry up."

Pascal drives off like a whirlwind. The wipers shriek on the glass, pushing away a load of water that seems to gather again immediately. Jo reaches out and taps on her sister's hip, but doesn't dare take her hand. There's rainwater running into her eyes and ears. She snorts like an animal, trembling with worry and cold.

Love Me Lili

"Did *he* leave?"

Valérie shrugs; the fat in her arms flops down, pathetic, against the embossed dress, too warm for the season despite the thunderstorm.

"I couldn't take it any more."

"So it was your decision?" Séverine insists.

"No, it was his, but he's right."

"You're saying he's right? Listen to yourself."

Séverine is upset and angry on Valérie's behalf, as if Valérie was speaking for all women when in fact it's only about her. She's leaning against the outside wall of the school, barely sheltering under the roof projection, one foot against a tub of flowers. It's still thundering, exploding in the distance. She lights a cigarette – the last one before going back to work. Playtime is almost over, and she's only taking a break because Valérie has dropped by. The teacher is bound to make an unpleasant comment when she gets back, because she's supposed to watch the children during playtime, but shit, she's exhausted. And with this rain on top of everything else, the kids are going to get water everywhere.

"There's no right or wrong; in any case, I was expecting it. I think I'd even been expecting him to do it for a long time."

"Then why didn't you leave?"

Valérie shakes her head and hesitates. "I don't know. After all, you know him, he's nice."

In fact, Séverine isn't really listening. She's applying every answer to her own case, wondering if she's better than Valérie, if she's at a standstill because life has something wonderful in store for her or if she's painting a black picture again and her life isn't so bad after all, compared to her friend's.

The phone vibrates and rings in the pocket of her work smock.

"Go on, you can answer it."

"No, it's my mother, and I've no wish to speak to her." Séverine silences the device with her thumb and draws a little satisfaction from it, confusing the machine with the caller. "You were saying?"

"I don't know any more."

"Are you going to find yourself a guy who can give you a kid?"

Valérie grits her teeth: Séverine rarely minces her words. Never, in fact. "You're kidding. It's too late now."

"You still could. You've got a few more years left."

In silence, they draw on their cigarettes at the same time. They'd like to sit down, but the wood of the only available bench is saturated with water. Its forest-green paint has been cracking for a long time, chips scratched off by the teenagers who sometimes loiter outside the school while waiting to pick up a sibling. There are words carved in the wood, and sentences written with a marker. *Porn to be alive*, for instance, the loop of the first B having been deliberately erased. Below that, *Love me Lili* – probably with the point of a compass – must have been long and hard to engrave, a true labour of love. Valérie sighs. She stamps on the spot and crosses her arms over her large chest.

"Things have been complicated with me and Patrick for a long time, and since the last building site it's become unbearable. So I guess it was time."

"Where's he going? Do you know?"

"Apparently he wants to leave here. He mentioned a public building firm in Marseilles."

"Marseilles? So he wouldn't be working with Manuel any more?" This separation seems to her more outrageous than the other one.

Her phone rings again. "Shit, can't she leave me alone?"

"Maybe you should answer."

It's the weakness in Valérie's voice, this compliance before an order, that prompts Séverine to switch off her phone completely. She stuffs it angrily to the bottom of her pocket. "Does Manuel know?"

"Not sure. I imagine he would have told you, wouldn't he?"

"No. We don't talk much at the moment."

They exchange a glance, friendly but not overly so; they became friends twenty years ago because their men were. They both wonder if it will carry on now that one of the couples has exploded. Séverine has kept a kind of adolescent cruelty in her friendships, a need to surround herself with people whose worth reflects well on her; Valérie's limp gentleness, her very body puts her off. They're no longer young enough for her friend to make Séverine feel good about herself, and her loser's face gives Séverine the horrible impression she, too, is one. But neither of them has forgotten the famous evening when Séverine once lost it. Jo was five, Céline six, and Séverine about to celebrate her twenty-fourth birthday. She was so young, and she was

dragging her daughters behind her like annoying append-
ages now that she had regained her shape and her desire
to go dancing. But nightclub sessions had been replaced
with dinners with colleagues, or rather her husband's colleagues and their wives. So she drank a bit too much and
laughed loudly, sitting outside the Cheval Blanc, while
bottles of rosé circulated among the workmen, whose conversations alternated between healthy anti-boss anger and
rather heavy-handed tenderness aimed at their wives. The
kids were playing between and under the tables, a few push-
chairs blocking the way, so the waiter served the dishes over
them. There was a fun atmosphere: the guys were coming
out of themselves, cheerful and letting their hair down.
But Séverine had had too much to drink, and when they
started playing a 1980s compilation – old stuff she didn't
even like – her emotions bubbled up to breaking point
without her quite knowing why. Maybe it was because of
those stupid hit songs everybody obviously knew the words
to, so everybody started singing "*et moi je vis ma vie à pile
ou face*" and then "*que je t'aime, que je t'aime que je t'aime*",
the guys yelling like coyotes, the women responding, and
when the owner came out with fresh bottles, he was yelling
as loud as them. But when they started singing "*Comme une
pierre que l'on jette dans l'eau vive d'un ruisseau*", she felt so sad
that Valérie noticed and came to sit next to her. The circles
of wine under the balloon glasses were tearing the paper
tablecloth, and Séverine was following the wet tracks with
her fingers, pulling bits off, folding them – focusing on her
hands so as not to start crying. And then Valérie's presence,
her gentleness – though Séverine was wary of gentleness,
a sign of weakness – and the kindness of her questions. So
she suddenly let rip like she'd never done before: she'd had

enough, she was anxious, she had daughters growing up who she didn't always want to look after, she wanted to go back to the lycée, and then being carefree, that was over but she didn't want it to be, it had all happened too fast. The feeling of missing out on her life but not knowing what kind of life she wanted instead. Twenty-four years old and life was already laid out. The drink, Valérie's attentive silence and the surrounding noise like a screen had prompted her to talk like she'd never dared before.

Although it came as a relief, the memory of it made her feel mortified the next day. And remembering it today is still unpleasant. Because of that evening, Valérie knows that for all her airs, Séverine has cracks like everybody else in this world.

"So are you coping?"

Valérie grimaces in a twisted smile. "I haven't got a job any more."

"What?"

"Restructuring. There's several of us, not just me."

"Shit. Bastards. What are you going to do?"

"I don't know. I have an appointment at the Pôle employment agency tomorrow."

"Yes, but aren't going to go after them about the redundancy?"

"I'd rather not rock the boat. They've given us a small bonus… If we start screaming and shouting they may never take us back. But, well, if I keep my mouth shut, then maybe next time they're hiring they'll remember me, right?"

A woman pushes open the door and calls Séverine sharply, reminding her that the children have been back in class for over five minutes. Her tone is annoyed, falsely benevolent and categorical. Séverine gives Valérie's arm a squeeze, kisses her and disappears into the school. Just before closing the door, she turns. "Drop in at home whenever you like. You're not on your own."

The promise makes Valérie's cheeks quiver a little; she lifts her eyes very high, presses her fingers into the dark rings and sniffs. She doesn't want her tears to flow, these large tears of abandonment and half a messed-up life.

Blood on the Sheets

"Where's Maman?"

Jo can't answer. Their mother must be stuck at work, it's what they tell themselves, it's the best thing to tell themselves, of course.

"I'm here," Jo whispers, wishing she was somewhere else, in the rain or still crouching in the rows of vines, anywhere but here, in this ridiculous pale-blue hospital gown and paper cap, with these doctors fussing over her sister who, legs spread and breathing erratic, is calling for her mother.

Céline is shrieking, clutching Jo's hand; neither of them knows how long they've been here waiting for things to happen without them, since nobody's talking to them.

A woman in a white coat slides a large, cold cylinder over Céline's belly, a thing connected to a machine that beeps and displays figures in red. Another one floods Céline's crotch with Betadine. They appear to think it's going to happen right now, they're saying that the cervix is dilated, and given the screams Céline is letting out at regular intervals, the contractions are close together. The gynaecologist finally arrives: they assume it's a doctor, judging by the sudden deference of the nurses as soon as he turns up. He slowly washes his hands, concentrating on every bit of skin, rubbing in the hollows between his fingers and his wrists, up to halfway up his forearms. He finally sits on a stool at the foot of the bed, without looking at the girl's face.

"It's happening, Mademoiselle. Let's pull ourselves together and get on with it."

Céline is crying, her nose running, she's in pain and she doesn't know what *let's get on with it* means.

The gynaecologist taps on her thigh, visibly annoyed.

"Listen … Céline?" He's stuck his nose into the admission record hanging on the edge of the bed on wheels. "You're going to have a baby, so either you get down to work, or we give you a Caesarian. It's up to you."

"What am I supposed to do?" she asks, her voice hoarse from crying.

"Haven't you attended any childbirth classes?"

Céline starts crying even harder. The gynaecologist sighs. He looks at his patient and at Jo, next to her. He finally seems to realize he's dealing with two kids; he gestures at the midwife, mutters a few words to her, she nods and adds a couple of notes to the file.

"We can't give you an epidural, so you'll have to be brave. But it won't take long. The baby's here, begging to come out."

"But it's too soon, isn't it?" Johanna finally dares to ask.

"Of course it's too soon, but if … Céline gets down to work quickly, we should manage it and the baby will go into an incubator. We're not in the 1960s any more, and I've delivered babies that were even more premature than this one."

Jo thinks the man's quite nice. Even if he looks bored, even if he looks annoyed at Céline's fear, though as far as Jo's concerned she's quite entitled to be terrified.

"I'd like to wait for my *maman*," Céline finally blurts out with a sob.

The gynaecologist looks at her over his glasses. Jo can't work out what he's thinking. Whether he reckons she's stupid or is thinking about his own daughter – if he has one, which is possible, he's their father's age – maybe he's judging her sister, maybe he's feeling sorry for her. Jo has a strong imagination and hostility to spare, she wonders if she'll have to jump at his throat, but would rather not because he's the only one able to help them, so for fuck's sake shut up and do it.

"No, we can't wait for your *maman*. You can do it on your own, my dear, and, besides, you're not on your own."

The bastard's clever. And the suddenly familiar tone doesn't shock anybody. Except perhaps the midwife, who looks up and frowns.

"If *you're* old enough to have a child, that means you're no longer a child *yourself*," she states categorically.

An especially violent contraction prevents anyone from replying: Céline lets out a throaty scream that extends into a push.

"Very good," the gynaecologist says matter-of-factly. "I can see the head, let's go again."

Jo lets her sister dig her fingers into her arms and squeeze her wrists until it hurts. Céline is panting violently. And then, in one last push, this time without screaming, she expels a red, sticky little thing which the man immediately grabs. Several white coats rush towards it. Jo realizes she's shaking from top to toe, and despite the stifling heat even her teeth are chattering as if she's freezing. There's blood on the sheet, she can see it clearly but doesn't know if it's normal.

Céline panics. "She's not crying. Why isn't she crying?"

A wail contradicts her. Not a scream, not the sound of a full-term child's lungs being deployed, not the sound of a victorious child who's going to rule the world. But a lively little noise all the same.

Jo strokes her sister's head; never have they been as close and alone as at this moment.

"It'll be all right," Jo can't help repeating on impulse – falsely conspiratorial, but not without hope.

Like the Song

Every so often, Manuel goes to hover over the incubator, which stands with others in a glass-panelled room not far from Céline's. He watches the tiny head he could crush with just one hand – strange, but he can't stop thinking about it: *I could crush it with just one hand.* This extreme fragility drives him insane, it's as if he's drunk even though he's only had two beers, he's thinking a thousand things at once and not knowing how he feels. He came straight from the building site as soon as he heard. His face, hair and clothes are studded with a thin layer of white paint. He can't stay still, paces up and down the corridor, returns to the room where Céline is slumbering, criss-crosses it, changing wall with each trip; he varies his trajectory but the room is too small for his movements. He looks like a madman or an animal in a cage. He suddenly sits down at the foot of the bed.

Séverine is here, too, she'd have liked to come sooner but she didn't know; she apologizes but not too profusely: if she feels guilty for switching off her phone she doesn't let on. She watches her daughter after seeing the tiny child in the transparent box. Sometimes, she glances at the TV at the tip of a steel arm above their heads, switched on but with the sound off. It's an animal documentary, first felines then large apes – a reassuring, banal kind of savagery. Séverine sits next to her daughter, on the only chair in the room. She scratches the seam of her jeans with the tip of her long, pink fingernails. She fiercely attacks the fabric. Céline would like to know what she's thinking.

But it's her father who speaks, all of a sudden, without looking at anyone. "You were pretty when you were born. So pretty. We knew it was too soon, we knew it would be difficult, but I was happy, you know, Céline. I was happy."

Céline is taken aback by her father's declaration. She wishes he'd keep quiet, it's too much, she's not used to it. He paces around the room, bewildered by the event. He's overwhelmed, and didn't expect to be to this extent. He's quiet now, and doesn't seem to want to say any more, and Céline is relieved. She hopes Jo will come back; she's gone down to buy Cokes from the vending machine in the lobby.

But when Jo finally comes back up and walks into the room with an armful of cans, she's not alone. A woman is with her, a woman who gives at once an impression of great weariness and great kindness. Ageless but attractive, a smile trying to be reassuring, her loose neckline falls over her shoulders and gives you the urge to nestle in its softness, in a wool you feel like touching. Her leather shoulder satchel makes her look like a student despite the grey hair among the brown on both sides of her face. While Jo hands out the cans, the woman shakes Céline's hand, then those of her parents. She says she's a social worker, that she has been notified by the school nurse, that she had been planning to contact them sooner but had had too much work. She says she was informed of the birth by the doctor from the Mother and Baby Council. She says she's pleased to meet them all. She says they're going to get to know one another but also do an assessment. Her voice is deep, a smoker's voice with a cheerful tone.

"What kind of assessment?" Séverine asks, far from pleasantly. Not at all pleased to meet her.

"An assessment of the situation."

"What situation?"

"Your daughter, and you."

"We didn't call you."

"I know you didn't. I work for children's social services and when such a young teenager gets pregnant, it's part of my job to investigate. Especially since the first report was made as a result of a beating."

Her speech is very polished, and she delivers it with warmth and detachment; this woman is the epitome of ambivalence. You want to push her away and be liked by her.

"Well, OK, but she's not exactly a battered child either," Séverine says, indignant.

"I don't know. It's my job to determine that, Madame."

"We've nothing to say to you," Manuel grunts.

"We don't need anybody," Séverine insists.

The social worker approaches Céline. "Was the birth all right?"

The girl nods.

"Are you planning to go back to the lycée, afterwards?"

"No."

"It's none of your business!" Séverine shouts. "Why are you asking her this?"

"Because it's my job."

Séverine loses her sense of proportion and raises her voice a notch. "You know what your job is, bitch? It's a shitty job! Sticking your nose in other people's lives… You think you're better than us?"

The social worker gives a little sigh, she's heard this a

thousand times. The change in tone, the aggressive name-calling. "That's not the issue, Madame."

"Oh, really?"

"I came to meet you, but I'm going to leave you all together for a moment."

"That's right, leave us alone."

"I'll call you to make another appointment."

"Get out, fuck off!"

"At your home would be good, perhaps."

Séverine is visibly swelling with anger but Manuel puts a hand on her shoulder to appease her. He knows social services because he also remembers Patrick's mother, and it's people like this woman who helped his friend, a long time ago. He knows they can be effective, sometimes even nice, but when they get the bit between their teeth... The law is on their side. So better not rub the social worker the wrong way, he knows that. Manuel isn't as much of a moron as Séverine might think.

The woman gathers her hair and twists it at the back of her neck, a gesture that makes her look younger than she is. "I'll call you next week."

After she leaves and the door closes on her and her unbearable calm, they're left behind, the four of them, for the first time in ages. Séverine is still angry – it postpones the unease and the moment when they will talk about what happens next. Moreover, it binds them closer together, having a common enemy. Even Jo, who dreams of running away, can't stand other people criticizing her family. Only she has the right to think they're total idiots, brutal or insane. Besides, she's never wanted to have a different family, just not to have one any more, and above all not to owe them anything. But she doesn't like it when a stranger comes to stick her nose in their business, it doesn't suit her. They don't need anything or anybody.

Séverine finally shuts up, squeezes the armrests of her chair with rage, and can't make up her mind whether to put her anger and the responsibility for the situation on her husband or her eldest daughter.

In the silence of her mother's hesitation, and since nobody has yet thought to ask, Céline announces, "Her name's Jolene."

Séverine then smiles. "Like the song?"

"Which song?" Manuel asks, but no one enlightens him.

Mother and daughter look at each other, assessing each other outside their conflict zone for a moment.

"Yes, like the song," Céline replies to her mother.

The Summer She Was Fifteen

He liked it that she was young. He liked it that he impressed her, he who didn't impress many people. Patrick remembers her back, the nape of her neck as she slumbered in the afternoon – the slumber of a child. The softness of her thighs, her moist sex. He didn't even do anything extraordinary with her, there were no buried fantasies he wanted to play out with her – she had been open to his appetites, willing, joyously naive. With her, he'd just felt less old, and had loved her like a teenager. There had been times, with Valérie, when routine sex, eroded by habit, had been replaced with a few more exciting experiences, variations supposed to reawaken their flagging libidos. But with Céline, he didn't need them, or want them. Her nakedness alone, her expressions of surprise and pleasure, the memory of a cry or a hesitation would give him a hard-on hours later. She was no longer his friend's daughter. She was just herself, and his. It took a lot of insincerity to keep up the pretence, to not feel like a bastard. Céline could be a bit stupid, a bit slow, answering his calls in a childish voice, calling her friends "bitch" or "my darling", relating very seriously some silly little conflict with a teacher. He sometimes found it annoying, it reminded him of his age, but wasn't enough to put an end to his addiction. Her smooth skin, her toned flesh, her enthusiasm. This obsession hurt sometimes, but it opened up a world in which he was the opposite of what he appeared: the opposite of a bastard, the opposite of an old fool screwing a little girl; it was just the possibility of being something else that she offered him, a glimpse of an inexpressible absolute, a truth that would never be shared by others – an undefined, yet essential truth that was much more powerful than he. With her, he felt better, as though everything could start again.

He's back here for the weekend, he had to see her. In addition, he has to pick up a few more things Valérie has been kind enough to store for him; she's kept the apartment. It's hard to afford the rent, but she seems to be managing. He hasn't thought about this topic too much.

He's arranged to meet Céline in the park, the one at the back of the town hall. There's nobody here at this time, and besides, it's winter: the slides are wet, the soil muddy, split by frozen puddles.

He sees her coming from a distance, wheeling the buggy in front of her. He sees her dark hair swaying as she moves, her new hairstyle clearing her face, her hips pressing against the buggy's handle. She stops a few feet away, seems not to want to go further, so he walks towards her.

The first time, it was she who had come to him, despite the fear of being turned down because she was too young. The first time, it was at his place, just after Valérie had left for work. Two days after the trip to Salins-de-Giraud, she'd appeared like a flower at the apartment. And she didn't even need a lame excuse, because they understood each other even at the door.

She thought a man's sex became rough, with time; the same way as hands and face become lined, thicker or cracked. She was surprised by the softness of his skin, the fragility of his testicles in her young girl's hands. She knelt down in the hallway and took him in her mouth, because that was the only thing she wanted: this male sex, smooth and hard, this point of pride for the two of them, he fully aware of his actions, she certain that it was because of her he had such a hard-on. And, for the first time, although she thought she had something to prove, she forgot about rules, meanings and pornography. Forgot what she was supposed to do and not do, at an age when these things are of paramount importance; desire alone guided her tongue, her lips, her hands. She rubbed her face against his penis in the same way a small animal nestles, played as if nothing was more important than the game itself; she didn't understand at all what was happening to her, she lost control when she was actually at the heart of things. All this desire made him tremble, he stroked her hair with his fingertips, pulled in his stomach for fear of being rough or clumsy, or of being caught. It was he who had made her stand up and led her to the sofa, afraid to come in her mouth. Maybe it was these moments that had determined the worth of their relationship, the one they decided to grant it. Subsequently, there had been other, very happy times, joyful sex and passionate fucks, but nothing ever matched the magic of that first blow job in the hallway, the magic as tenuous as a declaration of love.

Very soon, he stopped blowing his wages on bets after work, and started saving up to pay for a hotel. Céline loved that. She saw nothing shabby or sordid in it. The hotel was about clean white sheets and your own room, even for just a couple of hours. Her El Dorado was very much female. She also liked the fact that it was forbidden, and the difficulty of getting together. They met a dozen times, no more. Whenever they bumped into each other elsewhere, they didn't even have to pretend: they became other people, went back to being what they were supposed to be to each other, and without anybody noticing, a new complicity was triggered by these moments.

They didn't talk of love, they didn't talk much, actually, each of them living this experience like their own private film, with an inner interpretation of it that excluded the other. It was an exquisite misunderstanding.

He sometimes tells himself he let a man die *for her.* That's when the images come back. The rest of the time, he tries to forget. It helps not to talk about it. It was too hard when he was alone with Manuel. Especially since the night when... That's what he calls it in his head, no other way to refer to it. *The night when.* After that night, in front of Manuel, he became a piece of shit, a first-rate bastard. He was ashamed. It was far better to leave. It was the only way out he could find, and, all in all, it probably wasn't the worst.

Since he's been in Marseilles, he sometimes doesn't even think about it, neither about her nor about the body crushed by the burial beneath hardened concrete. Sometimes, he walks around the city and even beyond it for hours, wandering as far as Callelongue or the Baie des Singes. The presence of the sea calms him down. On the road to Les Goudes and at the very end of it he gets lost amid the sharp, chalky pebbles. Sometimes, he imagines falling. He thinks about the bottom of the water, the silence beneath the sea, the dark blue to rest his eyes. Patrick no longer knows how to rest. He sleeps so badly that he's forgotten about lie-ins, even on days when he's not working. The future no longer means much to him, the future just means tomorrow, and the time it gets light. Evenings when there's a match on, he goes to the bar and joins the gang of men at the Calenzana, a Corsican bistro down the road from him. In front of the large screen, among the others, he feels lonelier than ever but less empty. That's the advantage of bistros. Admittedly, he doesn't think much about Valérie.

He looks like a guilty child when he approaches the buggy. A bit of a swagger under his unease, his clumsy gestures.

She looks at him, but with empty eyes. There's only the two of them and yet he whispers. "I found a job in Marseilles."

She doesn't say anything, so he wonders if she's heard. He realizes it's crazy, she's bound to know already.

"Valérie and I broke up, you know, it wasn't working between us any more."

Ridiculous, he feels ridiculous. Tiny, a liar, not worthy. He hasn't spoken to her for months. He summons the memory of her laugh, of her bottom on white sheets, but it's no use: the child asleep next to her and the post-natal shadows under her eyes elevate her to a higher level. She looks through him. Patrick finally dares, his voice a little shaky: "Is she mine?"

She doesn't answer. He blinks and grits his teeth. He wants to pick the child up in his arms, what he's feeling is new, it's idiotic, but he still finds it moving.

"Can I hold her?"

An almost imperceptible movement, his hands to the sleeping child, wrapped up so warmly she's vanished under the blankets.

"No."

So he stuffs his hands deep into his pockets and keeps them still. He walks to the swings, then comes back to her, breathing heavily, afraid – the moron's almost happy.

Maybe, if she said *Stay*, he'd stay. Maybe he'd face his friend. Maybe he'd finally talk. Maybe he'd be able to explain his silence *the night when*. Patrick likes lying to himself.

"I'll send you some money."

She shakes her head.

Céline doesn't take her eyes off him. He thinks she's magnificent despite the tiredness, the pregnancy spots on her face without make-up, her clamped-together lips, the adolescent hooded top under her anorak, with its little silver stars. And yet there's nothing childlike about her. She has earned her status as woman. At a high price.

After a while, his unease grows so strong that he feels like hitting something. "Shall I walk back with you for a bit?"

She turns around with the buggy and he takes that as a yes. They walk side by side without speaking. On the main square, Christmas lights are flashing in broad daylight; shooting stars hang between the walls, and stylized galloping reindeer are pulling a sleigh. It would be more bearable if it was raining. Outside the town hall, kids are doing skateboard and BMX tricks, huddled in anoraks with hoods lined with fake fur. There's a poster advertising the function room and another giving Mass times. Patrick and Céline walk past the young people without paying attention to them and take the vineyard path that leads to the houses. She struggles a bit with the gravel under the wheels, so he says *let me* and pushes her aside gently so he can guide the buggy instead of her, not really giving her the choice. She puts her hands in her pockets and lets him. Patrick finds it moving to be responsible for the buggy and the child's slumber. They walk slowly, as though they're in agreement over how precious the moment is and need to make the illusion last a little longer. He thinks about that first time, in the hallway. It's a thought filled with light and sorrow. About fifty yards from the house, she puts an end to their stroll. "You'd better go."

He doesn't answer, drops his head then lifts it again to search her eyes, waiting for a pardon or a confirmation that it all did happen. He wants to tell her it was important, baby or no baby. He wants her to know that he also still carries marks, under his skin and inside his head. That he hasn't touched a girl since her, not for months. That he doesn't really miss it.

The sound of wheels on gravel: Céline is already far away, her back to him, heading home. He watches her walk away and doesn't know if he'll see her again. Not for a long time, in any case.

He's devastated – and also relieved.

Blaze

There's a murmuration of starlings, like a moving tableau, above the blaze. Manuel has gathered dry leaves in the middle of the garden and is using them to burn the legs of the Voltaire armchair. An opaque, grey smoke is rising in the approaching night. The racket the birds are making with every shift in position is deafening, an elegant swish while they're flying and then the loud squawking when they land, like thousands of pairs of scissors slashing through the air, cutting up the sky.

Another building job has started for Manuel. The swimming pool is done on the old one, the tiles laid so that bitch couldn't complain. By the time she came back, the work was finished, and the newly filled pond was lapping near the enlarged swimming pool. He pictured glasses of champagne and arms resting on the edge. He pictured the bitch's body under the concrete. He's been working on a new villa in Ménerbes for the past two weeks. He misses Patrick. He had no friend closer than him. But he understands why Patrick left, and he, too, sometimes wishes he could leave and forget what he's done. He wishes he wouldn't bump into his neighbour every morning and see her inconsolable mother's expression. He also wishes he didn't wake up every night drenched in sweat, his heart pounding. When that happens, he gets up and goes to watch the little one sleeping; it's the only thing that calms him down.

The police haven't been back. Social services have, on the other hand. Séverine keeps lashing out at the social worker. But, when all's said and done, she loves hating her and doesn't hate having a cup of tea with her once or twice a month and complaining about her working conditions and about how hard it is to be a mother and a grandmother before she's even turned forty. She's helped them get benefits and that's very useful, although Manuel doesn't like to think about that. There's never been a question of taking the child into care, so Séverine has relaxed a little, even though she doesn't like the way this bitch looks at their lives, and her smile whenever Séverine tells her about Jo's good marks at the lycée, that smug smile as if it's thanks to her.

The smoke is stinging Manuel's throat; he pokes the pieces of wood with the tip of a metal spade.

Séverine can smell the leaves and the wood all the way from the kitchen. When she goes to the girls' room – there are three of them now – to check everything's all right, she comes across her own reflection in the corridor mirror. She stops for a second and studies her beauty, pushing forty, the wrinkles in the corners of her eyes, the lines around her mouth from laughter and bitterness. The skin under her chin, smooth but already too soft. An internal lamentation starts inside her head, at once coarse and elegiac – time is giving her a kind of poetry she never knew before. She suddenly jumps because a door opens abruptly: Jo appears, holding a large bag, and hurtles down the stairs without looking at her. When Séverine glances into the bedroom, she stands leaning against the doorjamb for a moment, watching her daughter asleep, the child curled up against her.

Johanna joins her father in the garden. Without a word, she opens the bag, takes out a blouse and throws it into the fire.

"What are you doing?" Manuel protests.

But Jo responds with that strange look of hers, and since he doesn't know what it's all about, he decides to keep quiet. He watches as she drops the garments among the burning leaves, one by one. After a while, he hands her the spade and she thanks him with a smile before pushing the pair of shoes into the middle of the flames.

"Wait, you'll see," he says with boyish enthusiasm, and goes to fetch a small can of gasoline from the back of his pick-up truck.

Triumphant, he pours it over the blaze, which explodes and rekindles a dangerously powerful fire. Its flames turn their faces orange and warm them up at the start of this damp, freezing night. The middle of the blaze pops and hisses.

She laughs softly, so her father is quite pleased with his trick. He hasn't made anybody laugh about anything for a long time. He tries to think of the last time he did but can't remember; perhaps when he played at being a monster with his daughters and pretended to slide into the cement mixer as if it was an ogre's pantry. They would have been six and seven at most. He can't recall anything past that. In any case, it's been a while since he's also laughed, and now it doesn't feel like he's about to any time soon. Besides, he doesn't really want to.

Manuel is relieved to see the remnants of the armchair disappear at the same time as the pretty blouses he knows nothing about. She hasn't asked him any questions, so he respects her silence.

After a little while, the bag is empty, or almost. Jo crouches by the fire, grabs a few books with fine covers, brings them close to the fire, then moves away. She puts them back in the bag. "Spoils of war," she mutters to herself.

Crying rings out upstairs, a sign that the baby is awake and that Céline is going to start an exhausted to-ing and fro-ing down the corridor to get her back to sleep, trying to do the right thing, alternating gentleness and panic, angry shouting and nursery rhymes. Jo has trouble doing her schoolwork when the baby cries, and when her mother and her sister start screaming at each other over the child's wailing, but she never complains; she knows the time will come when she leaves.

She's waiting.

Manuel's phone suddenly rings, an incongruous tune playing over the crackling of the fire.

Johanna looks at her father, moving in the patterns of the fire, as he answers and listens. She sees him close his eyes and rub the back of his neck with his large hand. He listens for a long time, mutters a thanks and shakes his head like a child. When he hangs up, his hand is trembling and he takes a breath as if he's been holding it for a long time. He lets out a sob.

"What's the matter?" Jo asks.

"It's my father. He's just died."

Almost Attractive (Epilogue)

They're almost attractive when they leave the house to go to the party. Their mother is wearing new feather-shaped earrings and even Manuel told her she looked pretty, just like that, even though he doesn't say much any more. Céline has dressed Jolene up like a doll and is proud of her even though the little girl is wriggling in her buggy, already eager to walk. Her little golden T-shirt rides up to the middle of her tummy, revealing the adhesive tape of her baby pants, her soft skin and her protruding belly button.

It's Séverine who's wheeling the kid in a huge buggy – the girls are walking ahead, as usual.

Manuel is already drunk, having attacked the pastis long before leaving. Consequently, he's lagging behind, looking at his wife, wondering if she'll let him touch her tonight, after the party. And if he'll be too drunk to get a hard-on. Then he's suddenly moved to tears by the chirping child. He approaches the buggy, and babbles nonsense to answer his granddaughter. Manuel is a boat with a hole in it and an unsteady waterline, never very far from sinking.

The girls speed up, arm in arm, putting a distance between themselves and their parents. They've got their sandals out again, the heat is everywhere. Céline missed her appointment with the Pôle employment agency this morning, but there's no work for her anyway. Besides, her grandparents are relying on her for the apples.

Jo's decided to stay on at school. At the teacher and parent evening, they said she had potential. That she should open up a little with others, that she should be more trusting. It made her laugh.

They're feeling too hot and their sleeveless tops are damp. They can already hear the music and start singing – *Freed from desire, mind and senses purified.* Things that don't change can almost be reassuring, sometimes, as comforting as an old, familiar angst.

They sing loudly, stepping into this new summer by shaking their heads to the rhythm of the song, like a denial. Céline brushes a lock of hair behind an ear; Jo stuffs her hands into the back pockets of her jeans, emphasizing her dark shoulders and small breasts.

They skip, gyrate their pelvises, stifle a laugh: they still have a little childhood left, with its scraps of hope and its effect on the future.

They wonder which of them will suggest a ride on the Tarantula first. And who will get in with them.

Acknowledgements

Thanks to Stéphanie Louit, who was with me and supported me all the time I was writing this novel and all the ones before it.

Thanks to Cédric Tartiveau, who took the time to tell me about building work and the relationships between the guys on a site. Thanks to Jean-Christophe Tixier, for sharing my uncertainties and for his precious encouragement.

Thanks to Nicolas Mathieu, who provided the title for this novel in the original French, *L'Été circulaire*.

Thanks to Benoît Minville, who, as well as the aforementioned, kept the anger and impetus alive through heated discussions and a solid writing friendship.

Thanks to Stéfanie Delestré, who was the first to prompt me to write this novel and to see its qualities.

Thanks to Clémentine Thiébault for her reading and her trust.